He was tall and rugged-looking, wearing blue jeans and a bloodstained denim work shirt.

His grip was strong, and Tara winced. Her stomach fluttered and her knees started to tremble as a dozen different questions filled her head, all of them fueled by fear and confusion.

There was a number stenciled in black above his shirt pocket. The letters below it read WCF.

A slow chill ran through her veins. She knew exactly what this meant. Whitestone Correctional Facility was located a good six miles south of the cabin.

He glanced toward the bedroom doorway now, then looked at her. "I'm not who you think I am. Not even close."

"What?" Tara was thrown for a loop. She had no clue where he was headed with this. "Then who are you?"

"Matt Hathaway," he said. "Special Agent Hathaway to be more precise. I'm with the FBI." Those green-gray eyes were intense. Unwavering. "And if we don't work together from here on out, we could both wind up dead."

ALANA MATTHEWS

MAN UNDERCOVER

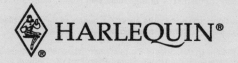

TORONTO • NEW YORK • LONDON
AMSTERDAM • PARIS • SYDNEY • HAMBURG
STOCKHOLM • ATHENS • TOKYO • MILAN • MADRID
PRAGUE • WARSAW • BUDAPEST • AUCKLAND

For Ann, Deb and Patricia,
who made it happen.

Recycling programs
for this product may
not exist in your area.

ISBN-13: 978-0-373-69475-4

MAN UNDERCOVER

www.eHarlequin.com

Printed in U.S.A.

ABOUT THE AUTHOR

Alana Matthews can't remember a time when she didn't want to be a writer. As a child, she was a permanent fixture in her local library, and soon turned her passion for books into writing short stories and finally novels. A longtime fan of romantic suspense, Alana felt she had no choice but to try her hand at the genre, and she is thrilled to be writing for Harlequin Intrigue. Alana makes her home in a small town near the coast of Southern California, where she spends her time writing, composing music and watching her favorite movies.

Send a message to Alana at her Web site, www.AlanaMatthews.com.

CAST OF CHARACTERS

Tara Richmond—The beautiful KWEST news producer who finds herself in the wrong place at the right time, and winds up hostage to three escaped convicts, one of whom isn't quite what he seems.

Matt Hathaway (aka Nick Stanton)—The rugged undercover FBI agent with a devastating past who steals Tara's heart.

Carl Maddox—A dangerous sociopath who has eyes for Tara and will do whatever it takes to get her alone.

Jimmy Zane—The brutal leader of the Brotherhood, a ruthless militia organization that will stop at nothing to destroy the government.

Imogene—The irascible old woman who helps Tara and Matt out of a jam.

Rusty Zane—Jimmy Zane's brother and coconspirator.

Lila Sinclair—The police detective who forces Tara to come to terms with a father who didn't love her.

Special Agent Abernathy—The one man Matt can trust. Or can he?

Chapter One

She was barely through the front doorway when a man with a pockmarked face put a gun to her head.

Tara inhaled sharply as her sack of groceries slipped from her grasp and hit the wood plank floor with a thud, its contents scattering: bottle of apple juice, ready-made chicken dinner, bag of lettuce and several oranges—one of which rolled across the woven area rug and landed at the feet of a second man.

This one was tall and rugged looking, wearing blue jeans and a bloodstained denim work shirt. There was a gun tucked into his waistband.

Oh my God, Tara thought. *Oh my God.*

Her first instinct was to flee, but before she could move, Pockmark grabbed her by the forearm and pressed the barrel of his weapon against her temple.

"Simmer down, now, cutie-pie. You aren't going anywhere."

His grip was strong and Tara winced. Her stomach

fluttered and her knees started to tremble as a dozen different questions filled her head, all of them fueled by fear and confusion.

"Who are you? What do you want from me?"

Pockmark kicked the door shut behind her and shoved her toward the couch. It had been several months since she'd last been to the cabin and a cloud of dust billowed as he sat her down. Hard.

"Easy, Carl," the tall one said. "No reason to get so rough."

"You're lucky I didn't shoot her on sight."

Carl ripped the purse from her shoulder and rifled through it, finding her wallet. He quickly removed three twenties, stuffed them into his pocket, then flipped through the card holder, stopping when he saw something he didn't like.

"Well now, ain't this the cherry on top of the ice cream. She's a reporter."

"Not a reporter," Tara said quickly, trying to keep her voice from wavering. "I'm just a segment producer. KWEST Morning News."

Carl tossed the purse and wallet aside. "Same difference, sweetheart. What are you doing up here? You own this place?"

"M-My sister. It belongs to my sister and her husband."

Susan and Kyle had bought the cabin three years ago, when Kyle decided to try the outdoor life. Mountains, fishing reels, hunting rifles, the whole package. Problem was, Kyle had never cast a reel or shot a firearm in his life and spent more time taking afternoon naps than he did hitting the hiking trails.

Tara, on the other hand, thrived in the outdoors and couldn't stand the thought of this place sitting empty. She relished the chance to get away from the studio and the cameras and all of the inflated egos she had to contend with every day, so she took each opportunity she had to spend time up here.

But the last thing she'd expected to walk in on was two strangers with guns.

Her whole body was trembling now and she had difficulty breathing. If she didn't try to calm down and assess this situation, she'd soon be in the middle of a full-blown panic attack.

Breathe, Tara. Breathe. If they really wanted to hurt you, they would have done it already.

Or would they?

"So you expecting sis and her hubby anytime soon?" Carl asked. "Or did you come here alone?"

Tara hesitated. Was that why they were here? Did they know that Kyle had money? Had they been expecting him to show up instead of her?

No, she thought. That didn't fit. This whole scenario had an impromptu feel. They hadn't been expecting anyone.

So who were they? And what *did* they want?

Tara closed her eyes. This wasn't really happening. It had to be a nightmare.

Please be a nightmare.

"Well?" Carl said, snapping his fingers to get her attention. "I can't read your mind."

"Knock it off, Carl," the tall one told him. "Give her some space. Can't you see she's scared?"

He was about six-two, with green-gray eyes, broad shoulders and a hard, sinewy frame. Under any other circumstances, Tara might have considered him good-looking. *More* than good-looking. But she was operating with a different set of priorities right now.

He bent down and picked up the stray orange at his feet, then crossed to her grocery bag and began gathering up the spilled items, placing them back inside.

Carl scowled at him. "What the hell is this? You the maid now?"

"This woman didn't ask for our company. The least we can do is be polite."

"Polite? Are you out of your mind? I'm trying to stay alive here."

The tall one placed the bag on the coffee table. "She's no threat to us. Why don't you settle down and go check outside? See if there's any sign of Jimmy yet."

Carl frowned. "You giving the orders now? That it?"

"Just making a suggestion."

Carl stared at his partner a long moment with un-disguised hostility, but the tall one didn't back down. Instead, his gaze shot past Carl and settled on Tara, and something flickered in his eyes, as if he were trying to send her a message of some kind.

Tara had no idea what it could be.

Didn't *want* to know.

Then Carl turned and looked at her again, giving her the slow once-over.

A shiver of revulsion ran through her as that pock-marked face broke into a slow grin. "I get it now. You're just angling for a little alone time with the lady. I can respect that." His grin widened as he addressed Tara. "You'd best be good to my buddy Nick here. He's been waiting for this for a long time."

Her revulsion quickly morphed into dread.

"Go on, Carl. Go wait for Jimmy."

"Sure thing, bro." Carl shoved his gun into his belt and headed for the door, the grin still intact. "You be gentle now. I want her in one piece when it's my turn."

When the door closed behind him, the tall one—Nick—turned to Tara and she instinctively scooted along the sofa, moving away from him. "Touch me and I swear to God I'll hurt you."

Her voice was shaky and high-pitched, but she meant it.

"Relax," he said, holding up his hands. "I just

wanted to get that hothead out of the room. You're safe with me."

Tara almost laughed. "Safe? Why do I have a hard time believing that?"

She looked at his bloodstained work shirt. He obviously wasn't a stranger to violence. There was a number stenciled in black above the pocket. The letters below it read WCF.

A slow chill ran through her veins. She knew exactly what this meant. Whitestone Correctional Facility was located just within Whitestone city limits, a good six miles south of the cabin.

"You two escaped from the prison."

"That's right," Nick said. "And things didn't quite go as planned, so we headed for the mountains. We thought this place would be deserted."

It was nearing winter season, and normally the area was a ghost town this time of year. But that was part of the appeal for Tara.

"I guess you thought wrong," she said.

She glanced at the gun in his waistband. It was close enough to grab.

Should she take a chance?

A big part of her said no, but another part wondered what she had to lose. She was, after all, genetically predisposed to recklessness, if her father was any indication.

"That's unfortunate," Nick said. "We don't need any more complications."

She didn't like the sound of that. Her fear kicked up a notch and her body once again began to tremble.

Whatever you do, Tara, don't make it easy for them.

Nick seemed to sense her distress. "Look," he said, "I told you, you're safe with me. I'm not going to hurt you. And I won't let Carl hurt you, either."

"That makes me feel so much better." She didn't bother to hide the sarcasm.

"All you have to do is sit there and be quiet. We've got help coming pretty soon, so we'll be out of your hair before you know it."

She was about to respond when a moan of pain filled the air, coming from the master bedroom.

Tara looked up sharply. "Who's that?"

Nick swiveled his head toward the bedroom doorway. "One of the complications. His name is Rusty. He took a stray bullet."

"Doesn't sound like he's doing too well."

"He'll live. But it won't be—"

Suddenly, Tara lunged forward, ripping the gun from Nick's waistband. Caught off guard, he stumbled back and Tara brought the gun up, pointing it at his chest.

It had been a while since she'd fired a weapon, but her father had been a career cop and he'd trained her well. Tara had never thought much of the man and still harbored a lot of resentment even all these months after his death, but teaching her how to shoot was the one thing he'd gotten right.

She was no longer trembling.

"Don't move," she said. "And don't make a sound."

"Put it down," Nick told her.

"I don't think so."

"Either put it down or pull the trigger. The choice is yours."

Tara had never fired at anything but paper targets before, but there was a first time for everything.

Not that Nick seemed too concerned about it. She could see in those eyes that he wasn't the least bit scared, and his confidence was unnerving.

"Go ahead," he said. "Pull the trigger. It won't do you any good."

"What do you mean?"

"Another one of the complications. There aren't any cartridges in that gun. There aren't any cartridges in any of our weapons. The creep who scored them for us didn't bother to give us any ammunition."

"I don't believe you."

"No reason you should, but it's the truth. This operation has been one foul-up after another."

Tara assessed him carefully. There was something about this man that didn't quite fit here. Something off. He didn't strike her as your typical escaped con. And she'd seen enough on the job to know.

Was he telling the truth?

When she thought about it, the weapon did feel lighter than it should. Concerned now, she glanced down at it.

The moment her eyes left his, Nick shot a hand out and snatched the gun away from her. The move was so quick and effortless, her hands were empty before she even realized he'd taken it.

She stood there, stunned, her brain not quite computing what just happened.

"Don't ever point a weapon at someone unless you intend to use it," he said.

Expecting the worst, Tara was surprised when Nick ejected the magazine and showed her it was empty.

"See? I wasn't lying." He replaced the magazine and shoved the gun back into his waistband. Glancing out the front window, he watched as Carl headed down the drive toward the main road.

Then he moved in close. Too close. She could feel the heat from his body as he invaded her space, keeping his voice low. "I need you to trust me."

Tara tried to back away but was blocked by the couch.

"Trust you?" she scoffed. "You're kidding, right? Why do you need me to—"

He put a finger to her lips, silencing her. "Because I want to know I can trust you, too."

She jerked her head back and frowned at him, but instinctively followed his lead and lowered her own voice. "Why?"

He glanced toward the bedroom doorway now, then looked at her. "I'm not who you think I am. And my name isn't Nick. Not even close."

"What?" Tara was thrown for a loop. She had no clue where he was headed with this. "Then what is it?"

"Matt Hathaway," he said. "*Special Agent* Hathaway, to be more precise. I'm with the FBI." Those green-gray eyes were intense. Unwavering. "And if we don't work together from here on out, we could both wind up dead."

Chapter Two

"FBI?"

Despite her fear, Matt could tell by her tone that she wasn't quite buying it. No reason she should. He had no proof. No badge to show her. And standing here with a bloody shirt and a gun tucked into his belt—empty magazine or not—didn't paint a reassuring picture.

This woman was yet another complication, but he couldn't continue this charade without her knowing the truth. Lying to two psychopaths like Carl and Rusty was one thing, but he had no desire to inflict psychological terror on an innocent bystander.

His own fear was threatening to get the better of him now, but he kicked it aside. Emotion was a luxury. He had to get her up to speed before Carl came back.

Another moan rose from the bedroom, and while Matt doubted that Rusty could hear them, he continued to keep his voice low.

"What's your name?"

The woman eyed him warily. "Tara. Tara Richmond."

She was a natural beauty who wore little makeup, and Matt had a feeling she'd broken more than a few hearts in her time. Not by calculation. Just through the sheer force of her existence.

She was, in a word, stunning. But not in that remote, overdone movie-star way. She had an athletic, girl-next-door kind of look that was hard to fake and impossible to resist.

He glanced out the window again. No sign of Carl.

"We don't have time to go into many details," he said. "But I've been working deep undercover for nearly a year now. Working up to this very moment."

She still looked skeptical. "So you're telling me the truth? You really are FBI?"

He nodded. "Through and through."

"Who are these people? What do they want?"

"Carl Maddox and Rusty Zane are members of a gang I've been trying to infiltrate for months. A homegrown terrorist group called The Brotherhood."

The fear in Tara's eyes deepened. "Oh my God. Do you think they're planning some kind of attack?"

"I'm not sure *what* they're planning," Matt said. "Two of our informants were murdered last year, so we've been running blind. The only way to get the intel we need was to put a man inside."

"Meaning you."

He nodded. "And I can tell you this much. These people are connected, well organized and extremely dangerous."

Tara leveled her gaze at him now, seemed to be weighing his words, assessing the story. He felt for a moment as if she had a tracking beam on him, her blue eyes searching his, searching for a flaw, a reason not to trust him.

"All right," she said, a slight tremor in her voice. "I'm going to take a leap of faith here and assume you're telling me the truth. But can't you stop all this right now? Can't you just arrest them?"

"I've spent ten months trying to get in good with these people, and Carl and Rusty are my ticket to the big show—whatever that may be."

Matt hadn't gotten a whole lot out of his jail mates, but he'd gathered enough information to know that the "big show" would involve high explosives, and a lot of them.

"That's all well and good," Tara said. "But what about me? I've got nothing to do with any of this."

Matt felt a tug of guilt. "If I could keep you out of it, I would, but my only option now is to make sure you're safe without compromising my mission. And I can't do that without your help."

She stared at him a moment longer, full of fear and dread and maybe even a touch of anger, and he found himself unable to look away. He was asking a lot of her and wouldn't blame her if she told him to go to hell.

He was almost surprised when she didn't.

"All right," she said. "What do we do next?"

Relief washing through him, Matt looked out the front window again, saw Carl on his way back up the drive. "We improvise."

He started unbuttoning his shirt and Tara's eyes went wide. "What are you doing?"

"Trying to make it look convincing. I need you to hit me. Scratch my face."

"What?"

"We don't have time for another round of twenty questions," he said. "Just do it."

IT WAS AGAINST HER better nature, but Tara followed Matt's command and slapped him, hard, across the left side of his face.

Matt winced, gesturing for her to keep it coming. "Don't stop there. You said you'd hurt me if I touched you, so make good on your promise."

But Tara didn't move.

This was happening way too fast.

Was he really FBI? Or was this all some elaborate

ruse? An exercise in fear and intimidation that gave him some weird, sexual thrill.

She'd said she was taking a leap of faith, but this felt more like a giant hurdle across a yawning chasm. She'd thought there was something different about him, but she'd never have guessed he was a cop. He didn't seem to have that self-important cop swagger she knew so well.

"Come on," he said, glancing toward the window. "He'll be here any second now."

Trust him, Tara. You have to trust him.

It was his eyes that finally convinced her. Those intense green-gray eyes. Unflinching. Uncompromising. But also full of what looked like genuine concern.

She wondered if he had any children. If he did, he sure as hell shouldn't be here now, risking his life like this for a job. Even if it *was* an important one.

But none of that was any of her business, was it? She had a choice to make. And the stakes were too high to say no.

Her heart was pounding, threatening to burst through her chest. Wanting to get this over with, she thought about her father again, and how much she'd resented him, then quickly reached up and dug her nails into Matt's cheek, drawing blood.

Matt winced and stepped back, grabbing his face,

swearing under his breath, and she immediately felt terrible, wanting to apologize.

When he recovered he said, "You're pretty good at that. Now you'd better get back on the sofa and play your part. If Carl doesn't buy this, we're sunk. He already has his doubts about me."

She nodded, then looked at his open shirt, noting the exposed ripple of abs. "What about my jeans? Should I take them off?"

He paused, staring at her. "That's up to you. I wasn't going to ask."

"If I'm playing the victim, I'd better look like one."

"I won't argue with that. You might want to mess your hair up a bit, too."

He turned away then, giving her a moment of privacy as Tara quickly ran a hand through her hair, tousling it, then unfastened her jeans and stepped out of them, tossing them aside. She couldn't quite believe she was doing this, standing here in nothing but a V-neck and panties in front of a complete stranger, but what choice did she have? If it meant getting out of this situation in one piece, she'd milk this part for all it was worth.

Feeling more vulnerable than she'd ever felt in her life, she climbed onto the sofa and scooted into the far corner, tucking her legs under her and hugging herself. She had been working for the Morning News for the better part of six years, but no story she'd ever worked on had prepared her for something like this.

She was trembling again. Before she realized it, tears filled her eyes and started rolling down her cheeks.

As if sensing her distress, Matt turned.

"I'm sorry," he said, and she could hear the sincerity in his voice. See it in those eyes.

Tara shook her head. "Let's just get out of this alive."

They held each other's gaze for a long moment— longer than necessary—then the door burst open and Carl came into the room.

Tara's stomach fluttered again, and she wondered if she could pull this off. But any doubt about that ability vanished the instant she saw a fresh new grin stretch across the creep's pockmarked face.

The sight made her shudder.

"Well, well," he said. "You two work pretty fast." His gaze went from Tara's bare legs to the scratch marks on Matt's face. "And she's a fighter. I like that."

Matt started buttoning his shirt. "Any sign of Jimmy?"

"If there was, you think I'd be standing here?"

"You try calling him again?"

Carl nodded. "No answer. He must be in a dead zone. Reception stinks up here."

"He doesn't show up soon," Matt said, "we may have to take her SUV and be done with it."

"Jimmy told us to wait, so we wait."

Matt frowned at him. "You do everything Jimmy tells you?"

Carl looked at Matt with what Tara thought might be a glimmer of suspicion. Or was her fear simply playing with her imagination?

"I don't know who made you king for a day, Nicky boy, but you get uppity like this in front of Jimmy, he'll put you down like a dying dog."

"I think you're forgetting who helped you break out of that prison," Matt said. "If it weren't for me, we'd still be counting the cockroaches on our lunch trays."

"If it weren't for you," Carl told him, "Jimmy's brother wouldn't be lying in there with a bullet in his leg."

Matt said nothing, but Tara could see his body tense. Carl had hit a sore spot, yet Matt kept his cool.

"We can argue about blame some other time," Matt said. "Right now, we have to figure out what to do if Jimmy doesn't show up."

"He'll show."

"In the meantime, we've got a search party looking for us and we aren't exactly mobile. Sooner or later they'll get smart and start heading for higher ground."

"We'll be long gone by then," Carl said. He grinned again and looked at Tara. "But right now it's your turn to step outside, bro."

Another chill run through Tara and she averted her eyes from his hideous face.

"What are you talking about?" Matt said.

"You had your fun with the lady. Now I get mine."

"I don't think so."

Carl stared at him. "I'm not asking for permission, Nick."

"And I'm not giving it. Not to you, not to Rusty, not even to Jimmy."

Carl's eyes went dead. It was clear to Tara that he was not a man who was used to being told no. "She belong to you now? That it? Your own private party girl?"

"Something like that."

"You know," Carl said, "I tried to tell Rusty we were making a mistake getting involved with you, and he kept telling me what a stand-up guy you are. But I'm just not seeing it."

The two men faced off, and Tara's heart once again began to accelerate. All she wanted to do was scream, *Stop it! Stop it now and get out of here. Leave me alone!*

But she didn't have to.

A voice boomed out from behind them. "All right, you two…back off…right now."

A large, pale man staggered into the bedroom doorway, one hand gripping the frame for balance as the other clutched a bloody towel to his right thigh.

Matt and Tara exchanged a quick glance. Rusty was awake after all. And it was a miracle he was standing.

A surge of panic shot through Tara. Had he heard them talking?

"We don't have…time for this nonsense," Rusty said, his breathing labored, every word an effort. "I can see all the way…down to the valley from my window. The search party is headed this way."

Carl spat out a curse. "You sure about that?"

"I wouldn't be on my feet if I wasn't."

"How long you think we've got?"

"Ten…maybe fifteen minutes max, depending on how efficient they…"

Rusty grimaced. Matt slipped an arm around him and guided him to a nearby chair.

"I've been trying to tell Carl that we can take her car, hook up with Jimmy at his place. Get you some medical attention."

Rusty nodded, then grimaced again and gestured to Tara, looking at her for the first time. There was nothing reassuring in the look. "And…what about our guest?"

Carl turned his predatory gaze in her direction. "Like Jimmy always says, the only good reporter is a dead one."

Then he crossed the room toward Tara, her panic rising with every step he took.

Chapter Three

Tara pulled back as Carl approached her. “Keep away from me,” she said.

“Easy, cupcake. As much as I’d love to drag this out, we don’t have time. So I’ll make it as quick as possible.”

But as he reached for her, Matt suddenly cut him off, placing a large hand on his shoulder and shoving him back.

“Leave her alone.”

Carl’s face grew hot. “You just made a big mistake, Nicky boy.”

“I just kept you from making a bigger one,” Matt said. “We need her alive.”

“What are you talking about?”

“Think it through, genius. We’ve got one man wounded and no ammunition. And with her dead, we’ve also got no leverage. No hostage to bargain with.”

“And who says we’re gonna need one?”

"There are at least a couple dozen cops headed our way," Matt told him. "You do the math. The more we stand around arguing about it, the worse our chances get."

Carl was about to protest, when Rusty said, "He's right. Back off."

Tara could tell by Carl's expression that he wasn't happy with any of them. Something very nasty was bubbling beneath the surface and threatening to boil over, but he kept himself in check.

Then he turned those dead eyes on Tara again. "Looks like Governor Rusty's given you a reprieve, sweetheart. But you make one wrong move, I'll execute your sentence in about three seconds flat. You understand?"

Tara nodded, her heart pounding again, knowing better than to show any sign of resistance. Carl had gone from randy sociopath to complete psycho too quickly.

"We need to get moving," Rusty said as he struggled to his feet again, then hobbled for the cabin door, gesturing to Carl for help.

As Carl crossed the room, Matt bent down and picked up Tara's jeans, handing them to her.

"Make it quick," Matt told her. And as she reached for them, he brought his thumb down over the back of her hand and stroked, a gentle, reassuring gesture that was meant to calm her.

Instead, Tara felt a small, involuntary stutter of electricity skitter through her, ending with a tingling in her scalp.

Was she blushing?

Pulling away, she stepped into her jeans and quickly fastened them, all the while marveling at the mind's ability to compartmentalize. Here she was, in danger of losing her life, yet that hadn't kept the hormones from kicking in the moment she'd felt the heat of Matt's hand on hers.

What the heck was wrong with her?

"Where are your keys?" Matt asked.

Relieved he hadn't noticed her little moment of embarrassment, she nodded to her purse on the floor. He dug around inside until he found what he was looking for, then he took her by the elbow and guided her toward the front door as Carl helped Rusty outside.

Keeping his voice low, he said, "I meant what I told you. You're safe with me."

But as they stepped through the doorway, Tara still couldn't keep her knees from trembling. She wanted to believe Matt, wanted to trust that he'd protect her, but with a nutcase like Carl on the loose, no one could guarantee anything.

She knew all too well about men and their promises. Especially cops. Her father had more blue in his body than a platoon of patrol officers, but where was he that night so long ago when their house had been burglarized? The night Mom got hurt?

Cavorting with one of his girlfriends, that's where.

Tara had only been sixteen at the time, but she was no dummy. And for her mom, her father's failure that night was the last straw after a lifetime full of disappointments.

The day after she left the hospital, Mom had quietly filed for divorce.

"Hurry it up," Carl said.

They headed for Tara's SUV and Matt took the wheel. Carl gestured for Tara to sit her cute little butt up front. "I want you where I can see you."

She was happy to do as she was told. She'd much rather ride next to Matt than be stuck in back with Carl or Rusty.

She was just strapping herself in when she heard it: a faint, but unmistakable *thupping* sound.

Thup-thup-thup-thup...

Matt heard it, too, his head jerking upward, staring out the windshield toward the afternoon sky.

Helicopter.

Rescue on the way.

Tara felt her spirits lift, then Matt said, "We've got a problem, boys," and jammed the keys in the ignition, turning the engine.

He was playing his part to perfection, which meant rescue might not be as close as she'd hoped.

Shoving the truck into reverse, he punched the accelerator and shot backward down the driveway, pulling onto the main road. Shifting into Drive, he said, "Which way?"

"North," Rusty told him. Tara's SUV was big, but he looked cramped back there, still clutching a towel to his leg and leaking blood all over her floor mats.

Carl leaned past him and clamped a hand on Matt's shoulder. "Just so you know, hotshot, once we get to the compound, there's no turning back. You sleep with The Brotherhood, you die with The Brotherhood. Got that?"

Matt swiveled his head, giving Carl a prison-yard stare. "Take your hand off my shoulder."

If Tara hadn't known who he really was, that look would've convinced her that he was just as dangerous as Carl. He still might be.

Carl must've thought so, too, because his eyes widened slightly and he took his hand away, leaning back in his seat, his fury still bubbling beneath the surface.

"Drive," he said.

As Matt shifted his foot to the gas pedal, the *thupping* sound suddenly grew louder and Tara saw a large black helicopter roar into view just above the trees.

MATT FELT A SMALL SURGE of panic as the chopper rose above them. The trees obscured his view, but he couldn't fight the feeling that they'd been spotted. If that happened, it was all over.

Ten months of hell for nothing.

None of the cops out looking for them knew who he really was. In their minds, he was simply one of three dangerous criminals, and if things got ugly, he doubted they'd bother to ask for his FBI credentials.

Not that he was carrying any.

Worse yet, his assignment would be compromised. Finished. And that just wouldn't do. He'd worked too hard to get to this point and couldn't turn back now. And while he knew that Tara was scared out of her wits—the last thing in the world he wanted—he had to look at the bigger picture and what it might mean if this investigation went south.

The roar of the chopper grew louder.

"Go! Go!" Carl shouted, and Matt punched the pedal.

The SUV shot forward, its beefy engine roaring as Matt rocketed along the narrow road deeper into the mountains. The sound of the rotor faded into the distance, then suddenly grew loud again.

"Take a left at the next fork," Rusty croaked. "There's a cave just big enough to fit us. Off to the right. We can wait it out in there."

Matt followed Rusty's command, guiding the SUV

off the road and into a ragged hole in the side of the mountain. Plunging into near darkness, he brought the SUV to a halt and killed the engine.

They all sat quietly, listening to the chopper's blades cut through the sky. It hovered for a long, tense moment, then revved up again and cut away.

Relieved, Matt was about to start the truck, when Rusty said, "Not yet. Let's make sure he's gone for good."

So they waited a full ten minutes before they moved, nobody saying a word. Matt listened to Tara breathing rapidly beside him and wanted to reach over and squeeze her hand, assure her that everything would be all right.

But would it?

Could he make that guarantee?

He knew that if it came to it, he'd lay himself down to protect her. Collateral damage was not an option here. But before that happened, he'd have to find a way to set her free, get her as far away from these psychopaths as possible.

How he'd do that without tipping his hand was beyond him at the moment. In the meantime, he'd just have to keep improvising.

Carl was looking out the back window. "We're clear," he said. He dug the cell phone out of his pocket and found it had a signal. He quickly punched in a number.

After a moment, he spoke into the phone. "Where are you?"

The voice on the line was just loud enough to be heard, but Matt couldn't quite make out the words. Then Carl said, "No, you can turn around—we've got wheels now. We took on some heat and had to bail. We'll meet you at the compound."

He listened for a moment, then nodded and slapped the cell phone shut. "They'll be waiting for us. Let's go."

Matt glanced at Rusty in the rearview mirror and Rusty nodded. Putting the SUV in reverse, he backed out of the cave and got them on the road again, heading north.

They wound through the mountains, following a circuitous route that Rusty laid out, turn by turn, until they were deep into a forest of redwoods.

As they came to the top of a small rise, Rusty said, "Stop here."

Matt touched the brake, brought the SUV to a halt. There were trees lining both sides of the road, so thick that they nearly blocked out the late-afternoon sun. This was the proverbial middle of nowhere, and Matt could tell by the look on Tara's face that she was as bewildered by Rusty's command as he was.

Glancing in the mirror again, he saw Carl dialing the cell phone. A moment later, Carl said, "Let us in," and, within seconds, Matt saw movement ahead, toward the bottom of the rise.

A man on horseback suddenly appeared on the road, gesturing to them with the rifle in his right hand. On his left was a large pile of timber, thick fallen tree branches piled just off the road.

As Matt pushed the SUV forward, the branches began to tremble and move, and it soon became clear that they were attached to an electronic gate that guarded a narrow dirt road. It was a clever ruse, and with the gate closed, no one driving along here would even know that road existed.

The man on horseback gestured again, and Matt pulled onto the dirt road. As the SUV bumped along it, the gate closed behind them and he and Tara exchanged a quick, surreptitious glance.

Matt knew that Carl had been right.

There was no turning back now.

Chapter Four

When she was eight years old, Tara got lost in the woods.

They'd gone on a trip to California to see Dad's sister Patty, who had a lakeside cabin up at Big Bear. An hour after settling in, she and Susan and Aunt Patty went for a stroll and Tara got separated from them.

She spent the next two hours wandering in the woods, terrified, certain that at any moment she would be eaten by one of the hairy monsters she'd seen on Thriller Chiller Theater.

At one point she found a narrow dirt road and decided to follow it, only to discover that it dead-ended. At the very end was a group of dark, dilapidated trailers that she was sure held something far worse than a hairy monster.

Human monsters, she had thought at the time, not knowing where this had come from. Something her father had once said, no doubt. He had, after all, dealt with such beasts most of his adult life.

Now, as she sat next to Matt, her SUV bumping along another dirt road, Tara was reminded of that time and wondered what waited for them up ahead.

More human monsters?

If Carl was any indication, then the answer was yes. But *Rusty* didn't seem too bad. He seemed more like a wounded commanding officer, in pain but stoic, not wanting to show any weakness to the troops.

Of course, that didn't mean much. Maybe when he was firing on all cylinders, he was just as maladjusted as his buddy Carl.

None of these thoughts did much to calm the beating of Tara's heart or the knot of butterflies in her stomach. She once again felt like that terrified eight-year-old, wondering when or if this ordeal would ever be done.

It had ended happily then.

Would it this time?

Matt spun the wheel slightly, taking them around the bend in the road until they came to a wide clearing that sat under an umbrella of tall trees. The sky was barely visible above them, a series of canopies with a camouflage pattern slung from tree to tree as if to protect the area from falling rain. Or prying eyes.

Over a dozen vehicles were parked in the clearing. SUVs, pickups, a couple of motorcycles, an old van. To the right, a large container truck marked RGB CONSTRUCTION sat with its rear gates open to reveal pallets of cement sacks and large bundles of rebar, the flexible steel rods used to reinforce concrete.

Beyond this was a cluster of squat gray buildings, a corral full of horses to the right and a lone horse hitched to a tree on the left. The animals stirred and huffed noisily as Matt followed Rusty's instructions and pulled up next to a black Humvee.

The compound was an incongruous mix of the past and the present, and all Tara could think was *paramilitary.*

The moment Matt cut the engine, Carl and Rusty opened their doors and climbed out.

Up ahead, a voice boomed from one of the buildings—"Welcome home, boys!"—and a large man with a crew cut, who looked like an older Rusty, emerged from the doorway, a tight smile on his face, a hand held up in a wave.

There were fingers missing from that hand, and the ones remaining looked bedraggled and burn-scarred.

Tara had once produced a story for the Morning News about a longtime bomb maker who was now working as an explosives consultant for the local ATF. He'd also had hands like that.

"A hazard of the profession," he'd said.

Crew Cut was moving to the front of Tara's SUV

now, shaking Carl's hand and pulling Rusty into a bear hug.

"I heard a helicopter swing by this way and was starting to wonder if I'd ever see you boys again." He pulled away from Rusty and looked down at the bloody towel pressed to the younger man's thigh. "Looks like you've got a bit of an annoyance there."

Rusty shook his head. "The annoyance is facedown in a ditch," he said, and the two men laughed, Carl joining in at the last moment.

During this distraction, Matt reached over and squeezed Tara's hand. No stutter of electricity this time, no compartmentalizing—the fear she felt was simply too overwhelming to allow for anything else.

"Stay put," he whispered. "In a couple minutes I'm going to get a little rough with you, so just play along, make it convincing."

How could she do anything but?

Tara squeezed back and Matt released her hand, throwing his door open and climbing out. Then the man with the crew cut turned, assessing him carefully.

"You must be Nick," he said, extending his mangled hand. "Rusty's been singing your praises for months now. I'm Jimmy Zane, Rusty's brother."

Matt nodded and shook the hand, but before he

could say anything, Zane's gaze shifted to the SUV, his eyes narrowing at the sight of Tara.

"What do we have here?"

"She's a reporter," Carl told him. "Showed up at the cabin after we broke in, so I figured the best thing to do was keep her close in case the cops managed to corner us. A little negotiating tool."

Rusty shot Carl an annoyed look. "Actually, that was Nick's idea. And a good one, too." He patted Matt's back. "Always thinking, this one."

Matt nodded again, then started around the front of the SUV to Tara's door. "And what I'm thinking right now is that we don't really need her anymore." He threw the door open, then grabbed her by the collar and yanked her out of the car.

Tara didn't have to do much acting. Matt was being as gentle as possible, but a certain amount of force was needed to make this look real.

She yelped and tried to pull away from him, but he pulled right back. "Why don't I take her into the woods and bury her?"

The words weren't comforting, but Tara knew this was merely a ruse, an impromptu attempt to give her a chance to escape.

"I'd like a piece of that action," Carl said. "She still owes me some alone—"

Zane cut him off with a gesture. "Nobody's burying anyone until I've had some time to think about this. So let's go inside, take care of Rusty's leg and get you boys up to speed."

Tara's heart sank, and she and Matt exchanged another quick look.

Then Zane headed back through the doorway, a man who was used to giving orders and having them obeyed without comment. If Rusty was a commanding officer, Zane was the general, and Tara's sense that The Brotherhood was a tightly structured paramilitary operation had just been confirmed.

Still playing his role, Matt shoved her toward the doorway and they followed Carl and Rusty inside.

A WOMAN NAMED ROSA patched Rusty up.

He lay on a cot in the corner of the room as she cleaned his wound and bandaged his thigh. Shoulders hunched, she rarely made eye contact with him, or with any of the other men who populated the room—many of whom also sported crew cuts and combat fatigues. There was a quiet sadness about Rosa and Tara wondered if she was here of her own free will.

Tara, too, was avoiding eye contact. Especially with Carl, who kept looking her up and down as if he were imagining that she'd just stepped out of the shower.

Bile rose in the back of her throat at the thought of this, and it took everything she had to keep from throwing up.

Most of The Brotherhood's compound was underground, an elaborate bunker with a maze of hallways that seemed to go on forever. The room they occupied was laid out like some kind of command post, a row of electronic gear along one wall, a large-screen TV, several chairs and a wide table that held rolls of blueprints, one of which was stretched out in front of Zane as he spoke to Matt and the others.

The TV's audio was off, but the screen was filled with a news report about the intensive manhunt for three escaped convicts, featuring mug shots of Matt and Carl and Rusty. The station was KWEST, Tara's employer. If they had any idea that her Friday afternoon getaway would turn into this, they would have sent a camera crew along with her.

It was funny, Tara thought, how being *part* of a story can change your perspective about news and news reporting.

Just a few days ago, her biggest concern had been securing interviews for tomorrow's dedication ceremony at the new Performing Arts Center. As the week wore on, all she had wanted was a night alone at the cabin. A chance to work through some of her grief over the death of her estranged father.

What a difference a couple hours could make.

With all this gear, Tara thought, Zane needed a lot of juice to power this place. She hadn't heard any generators or noticed any solar panels, but then her observational skills had been a bit compromised by the terror vibrating in her bones. Terror that continued to grow as Zane laid out The Brotherhood's plan.

"The days of McVeigh and Nichols are long gone," he said. "They got the job done, but they were primitives, with primitive ideas and outdated technology. We won't be parking any rented trucks full of ammonium nitrate in front of the target."

As much as Tara hated being here, as much as she wanted to bolt for the door and flee—assuming she could find her way out of the maze—she couldn't help but admire Matt for what he was doing. For putting his own life at risk to keep others from losing theirs.

But then she remembered that, like her father, Matt was a cop. She couldn't stop herself from wondering if there were any little girls waiting anxiously by the door for daddy to come home. Maybe he had a wife waiting, too.

"The plan's been in motion for weeks," Zane said, then pointed the gnarled stub of a finger toward the blueprint in front of him. "While you boys were killing time pumping iron in the prison yard, we were busy placing explosives near all the support columns in the basement and a handful of sweet spots throughout the building."

Matt nodded. "A controlled demolition."

"That's right. And we're the ones in control. You

have a government that won't listen to the needs of the common man, you gotta send 'em a message. You make it big. You make it loud. You make it deadly. That's the only thing that'll get their attention."

Tara listened as Zane launched into a semi-hysterical screed about the New World Order and the global descent into fascism. It had never ceased to amaze her how men like him could wrap their desire for mayhem and destruction in the American flag, when they were simply disgruntled little boys who like to blow things up, their ideals as hollow as their heads.

As Zane spoke, the others cheered him on, clapping and hooting after every second sentence of a speech that was nothing more than a variation of a dozen other such speeches Tara had heard over the years. She had no doubt that you could find the boilerplate version on the Internet. Whackjobs-R-Us.com.

It horrified her, however, to see that these particular little boys were so well organized and determined to succeed.

"We hold the power," Zane said, and suddenly the room was filled with chanting voices.

"We hold the power! We hold the power! We hold the power! We hold the power!"

As a chill worked its way up Tara's spine, she watched Matt chant along with them, wondering what was running through his mind.

Zane raised his hands to silence them and said, "We strike tomorrow, men. At 0900 hours."

"But where?" Matt asked. "I'm looking at this floor plan, but I still don't know what building it is."

A slow smile spread across Zane's face. "We're taking our cue from our predecessors and stabbing 'em right in the heart."

"Meaning what?"

"What you're looking at, soldier, is the Whitestone federal courthouse. And by nine-oh-five tomorrow morning, all that'll be left of it is a stinking pile of government franchised rubble."

The room erupted in chant again, everyone shouting, "We hold the power! We hold the power! We hold the power! We hold the power!"

And as several more chills rolled up Tara's spine, Zane once again cut them off with a gesture and pointed to Rusty in the corner.

"How's that leg, little brother?"

"Better than it looks," Rusty said. "The bullet went through clean, didn't do much damage."

"Good," Zane told him. "I need you over here for this."

Rusty frowned, then pushed Rosa aside and got unsteadily to his feet. "What's up?" he asked as he shuffled over to join them.

"Seems we've had a breach of security," Zane

said. "And I'm afraid I'm gonna have to hold you responsible."

Rusty's eyebrows went up. "Me? What are you talking about?"

"My man on the inside tells me that we have an intruder in our midst." The room was suddenly silent as Zane looked directly at Matt. "Isn't that right, Nick?"

Matt said nothing, but Tara thought she saw his shoulders tense, the muscles tightening beneath his denim shirt.

Something froze inside her stomach.

Zane knew about Matt.

"Turns out your new buddy isn't what he pretends to be," Zane told Rusty. "My man tells me he's Famous But Incompetent."

Carl stepped forward now, staring at Matt with contempt. "You saying this punk is FBI?"

Zane's eyes hardened. "That's right," he said.

Before another word could be spoken, Matt uncoiled and began to strike.

Chapter Five

When Matt sprang into action, all he could think about was Tara. He had to get her out of here.

"Go!" he shouted. "Run! Run!"

But Tara was barely on her feet when one of Zane's men grabbed her by back of the neck, causing her to yelp in pain.

Determined not to see her hurt, Matt lunged at the man, ripping him away from her and knocking him aside.

Just as suddenly he was surrounded by bodies, men shouting, hands reaching for him, fists pummeling, and he went down to the floor hard, steel-toed boots now kicking him in the ribs, each blow sending a jolt through his frame that resonated deep in the marrow.

In the middle of it all he heard Tara screaming, "Stop! Stop it!" Then a blow landed on his head and he went away for a moment, only to return when Zane shouted, "Enough!"

It stopped as abruptly as it had begun.

Lying in a ball on the floor, his body on fire, his breathing labored, Matt looked up to see that Tara was still in one piece, a trace of tears in her eyes. Another one of Zane's men had her by the arms and she was struggling against him.

"Let her go," Matt said between breaths. "She's got nothing to do with this."

Zane walked over and stood in front of him. "Collateral damage, I'm afraid. Something I understand you're pretty familiar with."

Surprised, Matt stared up at him.

How could he know about that?

Then again, how did he know that Matt was FBI? It was obvious that someone on Matt's team had sold him out—and there were only two possibilities.

Zane gestured and a couple of his men grabbed Matt by the armpits, yanking him to his feet. He kept his jaw taut, refusing to give Zane the satisfaction of knowing he was in pain.

Looking past Zane, he saw tears streaking down Tara's face and wanted to tell her he was sorry, to ask her for forgiveness for failing her. He tried to communicate this with his eyes, but as she stared back at him, she simply looked frightened out of her wits.

"Let her go," he tried again, struggling to keep the desperation out of his voice.

"I don't think so," Zane countered. "You're about

to get that trip into the woods you wanted. Only we'll be burying *two* bodies instead of one."

Carl stepped forward. "Like I said before, I wouldn't mind a piece of that action."

Zane swiveled his head toward him. "You think you deserve some kind of reward for bringing this traitor into our home?"

Carl faltered. "How was I supposed to know he's a fed?"

"Go sit your butt down," Zane said. "I'll deal with you in due course." And as Carl slinked away, Zane returned his gaze to Matt. "I fought for this country in two wars. Fought side by side with some of the men in this room. And we all took our share of bullets for Uncle Sam, only to come back home and find a place we barely recognized. Now you probably think you're some kind of patriot, some kind of hero, coming in here pretending to be one of us. But under the flag I salute, you're just a scum-sucking Judas who doesn't deserve to breathe the same air we do." He spat on the floor. "Get him out of my sight."

The men dragged Matt toward the door, Tara forced to follow as all around them the chants started up again.

"We hold the power! We hold the power! We hold the power! We hold the power!"

Then they were outside, the dense forest stretching out before them like an invitation to death.

"HURRY IT UP," the youngest one said, pointing his handgun at Tara's back. He couldn't have been more than nineteen, but his dead eyes outted him as a True Believer.

While she was certain she was about to be shot, Tara *couldn't* give up. Surrender just wasn't wired into her system. Despite the pain she had suffered during her childhood, she had learned from her mother that there's *always* hope, no matter how desperate the situation might seem.

Mom had battled a late-night attacker, endured a protracted divorce, practically raised two daughters on her own, but even during her darkest days, she had always managed a smile. And when she finally met Henry—the love of her life—she pulled Tara and Susan aside on her wedding night and said, "Always look for the rainbow, girls. There's always a rainbow."

So that's what Tara did as she and Matt were marched into the woods by three men carrying guns. Her face was stiff with dried tears and she was so scared she could barely walk, but she kept looking for that rainbow. Searched desperately for it.

It was out here, wasn't it?

It had to be.

THEY HAD BEEN MARCHING for less than ten minutes when they came to a stop in a small clearing. One of the men pushed a standard-issue military shovel into Matt's hands and told him to start digging.

That was their first mistake.

Matt squared himself and jammed the blade into the soft earth, tossing aside a pile of dirt. He was still aching from the beating and his ribs screamed in pain, but he refused to give in.

"Make it big enough for two," one of the others said with a smirk. Then the three men exchanged quick, self-satisfied glances.

That was their second mistake.

Matt wasn't about to give them a third.

IT ALL HAPPENED SO FAST that if she'd been asked to describe it in any detail, Tara wouldn't have been able to. All she knew was that at one moment Matt was digging a hole and the next he was whirling and swinging, using the shovel as a weapon, delivering blows to the heads and chests of the three men.

At one point a gun was almost fired, but Matt brought the shovel up fast to send it flying, then spun and jammed the sole of his boot into his attacker's gut.

Then all three men were down, Matt standing over them, breathing hard, and the only thing going through Tara's mind at that very moment was that Matt was her rainbow. Just like Mom had promised.

There was always a rainbow.

But then, as he beckoned her forward, Matt's eyes went wide. Tara felt a presence behind her, and an arm wrapped around her waist as the cold barrel of a gun was pressed against her head.

"You think it was gonna be that easy, cutie-pie?"

Tara stiffened. Knew that voice better than she wanted to. Tried with all her will to stay calm.

"Put the shovel down," Carl said to Matt.

Matt's face was immobile, but his eyes blazed. "I'll tell you what," he said. "You let her go right now, I won't kill you."

Carl barked, his laugh reverberating against Tara's left eardrum. He was so close she could feel the heat of his breath. Smell its stink.

He tightened his grip around her waist and pulled her backward a couple of steps. The heel of her shoe hit something hard and she glanced down, noting a thick tree root snaking through the ground. The butterflies in her stomach were back, worse than before, and she had to wonder if her mom had been wrong after all.

"What are you doing out here?" she managed to ask Carl. "Didn't your commanding officer tell you to stay put?"

"I'll be the first to admit I've always had a problem with authority," he told her. "Besides, you still owe me some alone time."

Tara could feel him grinning behind her. Could see

it in her mind's eye. Then he reached up and cupped her right breast, squeezing it through the fabric, pinching her nipple between his fingers, and a wave of revulsion burned a hole in her stomach.

Before she could stop herself, before she could analyze the riskiness of such a move, Tara jammed an elbow into Carl's ribs.

Caught off guard, he stumbled back with a groan, his feet catching the root. And then he was down, his face churning up in surprise and anger and humiliation as he let loose a string of obscenities—the particularly vile ones intended just for her.

As he raised the gun, Tara knew she'd made a mistake, she'd stirred the hornet's nest and no matter where she moved she was still a perfect target. But maybe, she thought, it was better to go out this way than to feel those grubby hands on her body again.

And as Carl pulled the trigger, she quickly made her peace and sent up a prayer.

But to her surprise, it was answered in a flash as Matt suddenly appeared—her rainbow, her protector—jumping in front of the bullet meant for her.

Then he was on top of Carl, knocking the weapon from his hand, pummeling the creep's face before he rolled over onto the ground, his upper left arm leaking bright crimson blood.

Tara cried out and ran to him.

"Oh my God," she said. "You're hurt."

"Help me up. We have to get out of here."

But he was big and hard and heavy and Tara had to use all of her strength to get him to his feet. And when she did, he staggered slightly, threatening to topple.

She threw an arm around him, letting him shift his weight against her, using her as a crutch.

"Your car," he said, patting his pockets. "I think the keys are still in it."

She nodded and they turned to head back the way they came, when suddenly a shrill whistle filled the air. They swiveled to find the youngest of their executioners up on his elbows, the whistle between his lips, blowing frantically to alert his comrades.

Matt slapped it out of the man's mouth, then Tara grabbed hold of her protector and guided him across the clearing and through the trees.

They could see movement ahead, a platoon of Zane's men spilling out of their barracks, so they cut to the left, pausing only a moment for Matt to catch his bearings. He seemed to be growing weaker with every step.

"Can you make it?" she asked.

"I'm fine, just move. Keep moving."

They circled around until they came to the parking area, but Zane's men were everywhere, weapons at the ready. The horses in the corral were braying and huffing noisily, fully aware of the chaos engulfing the encampment.

Reaching the SUV would be hard to do without getting themselves shot.

Matt felt heavier now, putting more of his weight on her, and she was afraid he might collapse. "What do we do?" she asked.

He nodded toward the opposite side of the parking area, toward the lone horse hitched to a tree.

"Can you ride?"

Tara didn't consider herself a woman of enormous talent. She didn't sing or dance like her sister Susan or her young nieces, Kelly and Kimberly; she wasn't as great with numbers as her brother-in-law Kyle; she couldn't paint a beautiful watercolor landscape like her mom. But there were three things she was very good at: she could produce the hell out of a story; she could shoot straight and sure; and like any girl who had grown up in Whitestone, Colorado, she could ride a horse like there was no tomorrow.

In short, the answer was an enthusiastic "Yes."

Before they could think any of it through they were circling through the trees as quickly as they could, ducking for cover when needed, Matt relying on her more and more to keep him upright, his arm leaking blood.

The horse was a powerfully built American paint

that shuffled and huffed as Tara grabbed the reins, hoping it wouldn't start. Slipping her foot into the stirrup, she climbed aboard and scooted forward on the saddle, straining to pull Matt up after her.

Matt teetered for a moment, grimacing in pain, and Tara tugged on his good arm until he managed to hike his leg up and over. Once settled in, he slumped against her back.

"Grab the horn," she told him, and he reached his arms around her. Unlike Carl, the feel of his body pressed close to hers did not send a wave of revulsion washing through her. Just the opposite.

But she didn't have time to think about that.

"Go, go," he said, his breath on her neck.

"Which way?"

"Doesn't matter. Just get us out of here. Now."

As she squeezed her thighs and dug her heels into the paint's ribs, she heard shouts behind them.

Bullets zinged through the trees, punching the ground all around them, and she frantically snapped the reins and nudged the horse forward.

Chancing a glance behind her, she saw several of Zane's men flood the corral and mount their horses. She couldn't be sure, but she thought she saw Carl's battered face among them. How he had managed to get back on his feet so quickly after Matt's beating was anyone's guess.

Remembering that greasy paw on her breast, Tara pushed the paint into a gallop and it careened through the trees, working its way toward higher ground.

Chapter Six

Carl Maddox rode hard.

He was angry. Didn't think he'd ever been so angry in all his life.

First, he's humiliated in front of The Brotherhood by Zane's exposure of a federal rat, then, to add insult to injury, the rat's girlfriend makes him look like a clod-footed fool. One minute he's feeling her up, the next he's sitting on his bony little backside with the rat right in his face.

And that, frankly, did not make him happy.

His only consolation was the shot he'd squeezed off, and he hoped he'd done some major damage.

Maddox could take a beating, had lived through quite a few in his time, especially in the army stockade back in Kuwait, when he was caught stealing from some of the locals. But he'd never let a woman get the best of him. Never even dreamed it could happen.

Once he got hold of her again—and he knew he

would—he'd make that witch pay in ways she could never imagine.

And take his time doing it, too.

One of the other men—Cameron—shouted something to him and Carl brought his horse to a halt, waiting for him to catch up.

"Jimmy wants us to back off," Cameron said.

Carl frowned at him. *"What?"*

"He says we've got more important things to do, and we're miles from nowhere. No way they'll get back to the city by morning."

Several more men caught up to them now, their horses whinnying as they slowed to a stop.

"What, is he nuts?" Maddox said. "I spent ten months in prison with that creep. I don't care if he's got a bullet in him, the boy is built to last, and his little party girl ain't no slouch, either. They'll do everything they can to stop us."

"Jimmy says shut it down."

"Oh, I'll shut it down, all right. But not the way Jimmy wants me to."

Cameron raised his eyebrows. "Are you disobeying a direct order?"

Carl nodded. "Damn right I am. Is anyone with me?"

Most of them remained silent, but a handful— at least five by Maddox's count—chimed in with a "boo-ya." As far as Maddox was concerned, that settled it.

"Tell Zane to start the party without me," he said. "I'm organizing one of my own."

Then he kicked his horse and shot forward, his compatriots falling into formation behind him.

TARA WAS LOST, had no idea which direction to go, once again feeling like that eight-year-old girl.

They had been riding for less than hour, but it felt much longer. The trail they rode seemed to wind on and on through the woods, with no end in sight. Tara had chosen it because it was the easiest, most accessible route, but maybe they should have stayed off-trail, where they were less likely to be captured.

Tightening the reins, she pulled the horse to a stop, then listened carefully to the echo of shouts and hoof-beats closing the gap.

She had gained some ground, but Zane's men undoubtedly knew the landscape much better and any slight advantage she had would all too soon disappear.

It didn't help that she and Matt were sharing one horse. The paint was strong, but Matt wasn't a small man, and if Tara continued to push it hard, she had no idea how long it would bear the extra weight.

"Why did you stop?" he asked.

The words came out in a vague slur. She had no

idea how bad his wound was, but he was still losing blood and should have been resting.

"We can't outrun them," she said.

"So you're giving up?"

"No, no, I'm just..." She tried to work it through. A thought was forming, half an idea. "If we can't outrun them, maybe we can outmaneuver them."

"How?"

Tara looked up through the trees. It was late in the day and the sky was darkening. They had ten, maybe fifteen minutes max before the sun was gone.

"Right now they're chasing two people on a horse," she said. "But what if all they were chasing was the horse itself?"

"A decoy?"

"Exactly. It might not last long, but it would give us enough time to hide, or hopefully find shelter, so I can get a look at that wound."

"I told you, I'm fine. I think it's only a flesh wound. Believe me, I've been through worse."

"That's good to know, tough guy, but even the biggest trees can be knocked down if you hit them hard enough."

"Where'd you get that from? A fortune cookie?"

"Back of a cereal box," she said, happy to find some humor in this mess.

She couldn't explain it, but despite the seriousness of their circumstances—or maybe *because* of it—there was something about Matt that made her feel at ease. Or, at least, the closest approximation she could manage at the moment.

Except for a shared glance or two, Matt had never been anything but business with her, yet she felt a kinship with him, a warmth, a natural, unforced camaraderie that, on the surface, seemed too good to be true.

Tara knew this was merely a temporary feeling. She'd produced enough stories about strangers coming together in desperate situations to know that, while they usually remained friendly once their ordeal was over, the bonds they'd developed were slowly eroded by time and distance.

If she and Matt ever got out of this, the weeks that followed would eat away at the memory, leaving only some silly schoolgirl fantasy in its wake. She wasn't quite sure what that fantasy entailed, but the feeling of his hard body against her back gave her a few ideas.

The hoofbeats drew closer. They had only a few precious moments to spare.

"If we're going to do this," Matt said, "let's do it."

With a grunt, he swung his leg up and over and quickly dismounted the paint, staggering slightly when both feet touched the ground. Steadying himself against the horse's hindquarters, he waited as

Tara climbed down, then swatted the animal hard, sending it galloping up the trail.

They watched until it disappeared from sight, then Tara slipped an arm around Matt and once again let him use her as a crutch.

"You're stronger than you look," he said.

"Is that an insult or a compliment?"

"A compliment," he told her. "You've earned more than your share today."

Moving as quickly as they could, they wound through the trees and crouched behind a tall clump of bushes.

With the trail still in sight, they waited, Tara feeling the erratic, nervous beat of her heart in her throat.

Moments later, six riders burst through the trees on thunderous hooves.

Carl was in the lead, his battered face full of grim determination, working the reins hard, pushing his horse as if it were a machine. His dead dark eyes sought out any indication of depressed earth or freshly trampled twigs before his riders streaked past and disappeared up the trail.

Tara and Matt looked at each other, both visibly relieved.

It had worked.

Thank God, it had worked.

"They'll be back," Matt said, and Tara noted that he was a little pale. Without a word, she undid the buttons on his shirt and pulled it down over his shoulder, exposing his wounded upper arm. He didn't resist, just stood there silently as she went about the task.

The light was waning fast, and all she saw was blood. Had no sense of how much damage had been done.

"Pull your arm out of your sleeve," she told him.

As he did, she grabbed hold of one of his shirttails and ripped off a narrow strip of denim. She slipped it around his bicep, just above the wound, pulled it taut and tied it with a double knot.

"We have to find shelter," she said. "I need to clean this. Stop the bleeding."

"No," Matt told her, pulling the shirt back on. "We have to get to Whitestone. Let my handlers know about Zane's plans."

"And how exactly do you propose to do that? We're at least twenty miles from civilization and we're losing light. There won't be much of a moon tonight, so we'd be stumbling around in the dark."

"We have to try," he said.

"You're in no condition to try anything. At first light we can start toward the city, maybe find a cabin along the way, someone with a phone."

Matt was quiet for a moment, and it was obvious that he didn't like this plan. "When we were prepping for the mission," he said, "we got some intel that The Brotherhood might have a hidden compound in this area. We did a bunch of flybys, used a thermal scanner to look for hot spots, but never found anything."

Tara nodded. "We once ran a story on thermal imaging. The tech told us you can fool the machines by using sheets of mylar. I wouldn't be surprised if Zane's compound is full of the stuff."

"I'm sure it is," Matt said. "But that's not what I'm getting at. At one point, we thought we'd found our target, but it turned out to be an abandoned mining camp. It looked like it had been there for decades."

"The Coldwater Mine. It was a tourist attraction when I was a kid. I don't think it ever got much business."

Matt scanned the hillside behind her. "I'm flying blind without a GPS, but if my memory is any good, it should be just over that hill."

Tara looked toward the steep incline. It wasn't an easy climb, but if they hurried, they might find a place to hide until morning.

Assuming Matt was right.

She slipped her arm around him again, and slowly guided him up the hill.

Chapter Seven

It turned out that Matt was only partly right. The miner's camp was not directly over the hill, but over another smaller one behind it, which they somehow traversed before the sun was gone.

There wasn't much left but a cluster of shacks, most of which were little more than piles of rotting lumber. Only two of them were still standing—if somewhat precariously.

A warped, bullet-riddled sign lay in the dirt near what Tara assumed had once been the entrance to the camp. The encroaching darkness and decades worth of erosion, however, made it difficult to tell.

The sign read:

COLDWATER MINE
Coffee and Sodas Inside

The mine itself was just a boarded-up hole in the mountain several yards beyond the shacks, atop a long incline dotted with trees. Tara wondered why anyone had ever thought they could turn this into a tourist attraction.

There was very little light when they made their way into the first shack, but it seemed to be in decent shape. It looked as if it might have been occupied fairly recently.

Someone else running from The Brotherhood, perhaps?

There was an old wood-burning stove near one wall, a small pile of chopped wood beside it and a cot with a ratty blanket sitting directly opposite it.

Tara guided Matt onto the cot, then told him to take his shirt off and lie down.

By the time he settled in, however, she could barely see him. A wan, almost useless slice of moonlight filtered in through a broken window. She could see edges of things, silhouettes, and not much more.

We might as well be blind, she thought.

Crouching beside the cot, she ran her fingers up Matt's arm until she found his bicep. Despite a growing chill in the air, his flesh was hot and sticky. But the blood seemed to be drying now, no longer leaking, and that was a good thing.

Probing the area, she gingerly touched the wound with her fingertips, hearing Matt's sharp intake of breath as the muscle tensed.

"Sorry," she said.

He shrugged. "It's just an arm. Not like I really use it for anything."

She smiled. "So you're a comedian *and* a tough guy. How impressive."

"Wouldn't want to disappoint you."

Tara carefully pressed the wound, unable to feel the hardness of a bullet. Maybe Matt was right and it was only a flesh wound, but she couldn't be sure without light.

"I wish I could see," she said. "There have to be some matches around here somewhere."

"Try the stove. I don't think it's been that long since someone was living here."

Tara slowly made her way across the dilapidated floor on hands and knees. She found the stove and patted the area around it, coming up empty.

"Nothing," she said.

"Keep trying."

So she tried again, still finding nothing, her frustration rising. She was about to turn away when her hand brushed against something solid, sent it toppling. She quickly reached out, groped for it and caught it just before it hit the floor.

A lamp. A kerosene lamp.

She picked it up, shook it, found that there was still fluid inside. Which was all well and good, but without matches, it was useless.

Setting the lamp aside, Tara took one last lap

around the track and ran her hands up the sides of the stove.

There it was, an indentation carved into the iron, carrying a small, oblong box.

Tara removed the box, heard the rattle of matchsticks, surprised that something so simple could bring her such a feeling of triumph. But she felt it nevertheless, another rainbow spreading through her, a tiny but significant sliver of hope.

She knew this was an overreaction, brought to her courtesy of what might well be the worst day of her entire life, but that didn't matter. She allowed herself to enjoy this moment. To revel in it.

They had escaped. They were safe.

And now they had light.

Tara opened the box and struck one of the matches. Reaching for the lamp, she removed the chimney and put the flame to the wick, then adjusted the level until the lamp burned brightly.

Replacing the chimney, she grabbed the light by its handle and turned around. "Ta-da!"

But her smile faded as she realized Matt's eyes were closed, his bare chest gently rising and falling.

He was asleep.

She crouched next to the cot again and brought the lamp close to his wound. It was a nasty gash and would probably need stitches, but it was nothing life threatening.

Matt's skin glowed in the light. She held the lamp over him for a moment, staring unabashedly at his muscular frame, noting a thin scar along his abdomen.

Appendix?

Something deadlier?

Believe me, he'd said, *I've been through worse.*

Feeling a small but familiar tingle inside her, Tara resisted the urge to reach out and touch the scar. It seemed to be begging for her to run her fingers along it, just as she'd run them along his arm, searching for his wound.

But she didn't act on the impulse. Dropped her free hand to her side and kept it there.

He's a stranger, she told herself. *You barely know him.*

But he wasn't a *complete* stranger, was he? There was that feeling of kinship she'd felt earlier, and in the past few hours, Matt had proven himself to be thoughtful and kind and courageous. An inner beauty that more than matched the handsome, rugged exterior.

He didn't seem to be a creature of ego. He simply was what he was: a man who did his job and kept his promises.

And she felt safe with him.

Protected.

What more could she want?

Tara had spent her entire adult life dating men who turned out to be much less than what she had hoped for. She had developed a pattern of attraction that seemed to reflect her animosity for her father. Had fallen in and out of love with men who showered her with attention, blissfully ignoring the fact that this attention had little to do with who she was as a woman, and everything to do with the desire to share her bed.

She had never given herself away easily, and when she did succumb, she hadn't always regretted it—she had needs and desires equally as strong as theirs. But unlike her mother, she had never found her Henry.

That one perfect match.

Her soul mate.

And while her mother was proof that it *could* happen, Tara began to believe that it may never happen for her.

Was she too picky?

Should she have simply settled for less in hopes that it would grow into something more?

Should she have said yes when Ron the newscaster had asked her to move in? Or when Eric the architect had halfheartedly suggested they marry? Neither of them were even remotely like her father, but neither of them had occupied a place in her heart the way she had hoped they would.

Those relationships lasted months rather than

years, and Tara blamed herself for that. Weeks in, she had felt as if she were pretending, only going through the motions because that was what was expected of her.

But she wasn't happy. Hadn't felt that twinge of satisfaction she knew she should be feeling whenever she was around these men. Whenever she thought of them.

So the search for her fantasy man continued.

And as she stood there, crouched over Matt, staring at his perfectly muscled body in the warm lamplight, she wondered, for the just the briefest of moments, if she had found him.

It was a ridiculous notion, of course, born out of stress and fear and hardship, but in that one brief moment, something swelled in her heart. Something warm. Exciting. A vague yet unmistakable feeling of...

What?

Fulfillment?

But that moment was gone as quickly as it came and Tara had to remind herself once again what Matt did for a living and how that kind of man had nearly ruined her childhood. If it hadn't been for her mother's strength, her mother's unending optimism and love, Tara would probably be a basketcase right now.

The day her father died, she made a vow to herself, finally bringing to the surface a thought she had carried in her subconscious for years: that she would never allow herself to fall for a man like him. Would never subject herself to a life of waiting and worrying and wondering.

When will he come home?

Will he come home?

She could not and would not go through that.

As she lowered the lamp, Matt stirred and opened those green-gray eyes.

He silently studied her in the lamplight, and she couldn't be sure he was fully awake. Wasn't quite sure if he was seeing *her,* or some phantom from a dream.

Smiling slightly, he reached up and touched the side of her face, using his thumb to wipe away a smudge of dirt or blood.

Tara thought it was one of the most intimate gestures she'd ever experienced. Her heart swelled again, and she felt an unmistakable stirring in her loins. That same feeling of desire that overcame her as she'd stared at his scar. She wanted to lean forward, to kiss him, taste his lips, feel his tongue brushing against hers....

But then he lowered the hand and closed his eyes again. Fell back asleep. She wondered for a moment if she, too, was asleep. Was seeing phantoms of her own.

No, she could still feel the warmth of that hand

on her cheek. Could still see those green-gray eyes staring up at her.

But with great reluctance, she dismissed it all from her mind, knowing this was something that wasn't meant to be. Like Ron the Newscaster and Eric the Architect, she would be remembering him as Matt the Cop and regretting she'd ever gotten involved with him.

Hating herself for it.

Better to stop now before it started. Fewer casualties that way.

Setting the lamp on the floor, she removed the tourniquet above his bicep, then tore another strip of his shirt and used it to cover the wound. It wasn't close to being clean, but she figured it was better than nothing. And tomorrow, when they reached the city, he could be properly taken care of.

When she was done, it occurred to her that this place, this ramshackle structure, gave them only the illusion of safety. If she and Matt knew about the mine, then there was a good chance that the others did, too.

Moving to the window, she decided that her time here would be better spent standing vigil. Watching the darkness.

Watching for Carl.

And The Brotherhood.

Chapter Eight

"How long was I asleep?" Matt asked.

It took Tara a moment to answer. "Not long. Less than an hour, I think."

The cot groaned beneath Matt as he fought his way through the cobwebs in his head and sat up. His arm was throbbing. Felt stiff and brittle. But the nap had rejuvenated him a bit and he was feeling stronger now. Not one hundred percent, but definitely a good three-quarters of the way there.

Ten months in prison had taught him the value of power naps. Getting a full eight hours was next to impossible when you're surrounded by a constant barrage of taunts and threats and, sometimes, shouts of pain.

Tara stood at the window, her gaze on the campground beyond. The past few hours had gone by so fast, he'd almost forgotten how stunning she was.

He vaguely remembered seeing her face in a dream and reaching out to touch it, thinking he might have died and that she was his guardian angel, here to guide him to heaven.

Matt wasn't sure he even *believed* in heaven, but if it did exist and he was lucky enough one day to be headed that way, he wouldn't mind having Tara as his traveling companion.

But then this brought up thoughts of violence and death and, if he had anything to say about it, nobody would be dying tonight.

He'd seen his share of death, had struggled for years to come to terms with it, and had no desire to repeat that struggle.

Tara was an innocent. A bystander. And he would do everything he could to keep her safe.

Assuming he could stay awake.

"Sorry for passing out on you," he said.

Tara turned now, facing him. She had smudges of dirt and a few specks of blood on her face and clothes, but this didn't mar the image. "You're kidding, right? I'm surprised you didn't pass out on the back of that horse."

He shrugged. "I had a beautiful woman to prop me up."

He was fairly certain this wasn't the first time she'd heard such a compliment, but you wouldn't know it by her reaction. "Are you sure that bullet didn't graze your skull, too?"

He offered her a small laugh in response and she

joined in, a short retreat from the seriousness of their situation.

Then Matt sobered and nodded toward the window. "They've found the horse by now. They're out there looking for us."

She nodded. "I've been waiting. Not that I'll know what to do if they show up."

He gestured to the lamp. "I don't suppose there's enough fuel in this thing to help us find someone with a phone?"

"I wouldn't want to chance it unless we're forced to. And I wouldn't want to be stuck out there without light."

Matt was itching to get moving, itching to let his people know what The Brotherhood was up to, but she was right. Unless Carl and his cronies found them, they'd have to stay here until morning.

Hopefully that wouldn't be too late.

Zane had said that detonation of the federal courthouse was scheduled for nine o'clock, but that plan might have changed in reaction to their escape.

There was also the question of who to tell. There were only two people who knew what Matt was up to. Only two people who knew that the ten months he spent in prison were a sham. And one of those two people had just given him up to Zane.

He looked toward the window. "I guess if they

do show up, there's no point in making it easy for them."

He leaned over and blew the lamp out, plunging them into near darkness. Rising from the cot, he flexed his bicep slightly, feeling the sting of the wound, then crossed the room and joined her at the window.

"You must be exhausted," he said. "Let me take over for a while."

"I'm too keyed up to sleep."

He could barely see her in the moonlight, but now that he was up close, he sensed that she was shivering. He was shirtless, and not exactly warm and toasty himself, and he briefly entertained the thought of slipping an arm around her and pulling her close to generate to some heat. But however good-natured the gesture was, it might not be welcomed.

And he had to admit that his motives weren't completely pure.

Instead, he grabbed the tattered blanket that lay atop the cot and draped it over her shoulders.

She watched the darkness beyond the window again, clutching the blanket tighter against her body.

Her eyes reflected the pale moonlight and he thought he saw tears in them.

"You okay?"

It was a stupid question. How could she possibly

be okay after what they'd been through? What they were *still* going through? But it would've been awkward to stand there and watch her cry without saying something.

"It's silly," she said, "but I was just thinking about my nieces."

"Nieces?"

"Kelly and Kimberly. They're four years old. Twins. Called me the other night and asked me if I'd come watch them sing at the new Performing Arts Center tomorrow. I promised I would." She paused. "I guess that's out of the question now."

"Don't worry," Matt said. "You'll make it up to them."

She laughed mirthlessly, a tinge of bitterness to her voice. "Where have I heard that one before?"

Then she retreated from the window, leaned against the adjacent wall and slid to the floor. "I guess I'm no better than my father."

Matt sat down next to her. Knew that the events of the day had begun to overwhelm her, and figured the best course of action was to simply let her talk.

"He made promises all the time," she said. "But I can't count on one hand how many he kept. He always had trouble with the follow-through."

"You were taken hostage by three escaped convicts. I'm sure your nieces will understand."

"My father had good excuses, too, but I never

understood. All I knew was that he wasn't there when I needed him to be. After a while I just gave up, and he quit pretending."

"Pretending?"

"To love me. To care about me. And I don't want Kelly and Kimberly to think I don't care about them."

"Sounds to me as if you love them too much to let that happen."

She nodded. "Susan's done a wonderful job. They're almost like my own."

"Then I guess it's safe to assume you don't have any children?"

Another mirthless laugh. "No children, no husband. Just work." She shook her head. "Don't get me wrong, I love my job, but sometimes—I don't know—I just get that ache. A house in the suburbs, two-point-five kids, someone to share my life with... My mom was disappointed the first time around, but she finally got it right. And I guess I want that, too." She paused. "But listen to me, crying in my beer. What about you? Do you have a family?"

"Two healthy parents and three brothers," Matt said.

"Older or younger?"

"I'm the oldest. About six years ahead of the others. And when I decided to go into law enforcement, they followed in my footsteps."

"Oh?"

"Mark and Evan are working together as sheriff's deputies out in Fort Worth, and the youngest, Sam, is on the SWAT team in Los Angeles."

"That's a lot of broken hearts," she said.

Matt frowned. "What do you mean?"

"My father was a cop, too. And the only time he ever paid attention to me was when he wanted to show me off to his friends. 'Look at the pretty little thing I created. Isn't she a cutie?' He was the same with my sister Susan. If he could've bronzed us, he would've put us on his shelf with his bowling trophies." She drew in her bottom lip. "He really screwed up, you know?"

"I'm sure it wasn't intentional."

"Oh? The straw-and-the-camel's-back moment came when I was about sixteen. It was a Friday night and Susan and I were out on dates, when some guy broke into the house, assaulted Mom on the sofa. Would've raped her, too, if I hadn't come home and pepper sprayed the creep. He took off and she wound up in the hospital."

"Jeez," Matt said. "And where was your father? On the job?"

"That might've been a decent excuse. Better than the one we found out about a couple months later."

"Which was?"

"Turned out he was sleeping with his partner at the

time. A woman who had the gall to sit at our table for Thanksgiving dinner."

Matt was silent for a moment. Then he said, "I can understand your anger. I really can. And I know you got a raw deal. But what does any of that have to do with my brothers and me?"

"They're cops. You're a cop. You're all the same."

There was a bitterness in her voice that was hard to ignore. A hurt. But he couldn't let her statement go unchecked.

"You're using an awfully broad brush, Tara. Not all cops are like that. *I'm* not like that."

"Maybe," she said. "But what does that prove? You don't have a wife and kids waiting for you at home."

Matt knew she didn't mean anything by this. Knew that it was coming from a place of pain. And exhaustion. But she had managed to insult him and stir up unwanted memories at the same time, and he couldn't help himself, couldn't keep the heat from rising in his chest.

He thought about what Zane had said to him earlier.

Collateral Damage. Something I understand you're pretty familiar with.

Barely controlling his anger, the words were out of his mouth before he had a chance to stop them.

"You're right," he told her. "I *don't* have anyone waiting for me at home. Not anymore."

She was silent as it sank in. "Anymore?"

Matt took a breath, not wanting to say it. He didn't like saying it. Never had, never would.

"My wife and daughter are dead."

Chapter Nine

Six words.

Six simple words.

Separately they meant nothing, but hearing them strung together into a sentence—into *that* particular sentence—delivered a devastating blow to Tara's chest.

My wife and daughter are dead.

Dead.

Like anyone, Tara had felt foolish many times in her life, but she didn't think she'd ever felt it with quite the same intensity as she did at that moment.

Foolish. Absurdly so.

And guilty. There was a pretty fair amount of that thrown in, as well.

My wife and daughter are dead.

What do you say when someone tells you something like that?

Tara had bid farewell to a number of friends in her time—a girlfriend with breast cancer, a coworker hit by a car—and her father's death had not been a picnic by any means. But anything she said to Matt in response to those words would be woefully inadequate.

She tried anyway.

"I'm so sorry," she managed, peering at him through the darkness in an attempt to gauge the level of his anger, the depth of his pain.

But she couldn't see him well enough. Could only sense that he wasn't happy with her at the moment.

And who could blame him?

She felt ashamed. "Look," she said, "I didn't mean to—"

"Forget it. You didn't know. There's no way you could have."

"That doesn't make me any less of a jerk."

"You're *not* a jerk," he said, his tone softening. "Far from it."

Tara should have left it at that and said nothing more. Maybe she could blame her background in news gathering for what came next out of her mouth, but she knew that it was really just simple curiosity and impulse that made her ask him.

"What happened to them? How did they…"

She couldn't bring herself to finish the question, and Matt was silent long enough to make her wonder if she should have kept her mouth shut. Then she felt him shift around and move in closer to her, leaning his back against the wall.

He sighed, and the tension in the air seemed to evaporate.

"I'm not sure the details matter," he said. "I spent half of the last seven years trying to forget them, then the other half trying to remember. The experts always tell you that once you've grieved you have to find a way to move on. But everything I've done with my life since then has been dedicated to their memory, so I guess the details *are* important and always will be."

"Listen," Tara said, "if you'd rather not talk about this…"

"Normally I wouldn't. But after ten months undercover, it's kind of nice to be able to let loose without filtering everything you say."

He shifted again, readjusting his position against the wall as if he were somehow bracing himself for the story he was about to tell.

Tara felt the sudden need to brace herself, too.

Then he said, "I'd known Becky since high school. Austin, Texas. We flirted back then, but it wasn't until a summer home from college that we got to know each other. We'd both been through breakups, and just naturally drifted together. And before we knew it, we were out of school and married and Jennifer was born."

He was silent, as if lost in the memory, and Tara had the urge to reach over, take his hand in hers and squeeze it the way he'd squeezed hers in the car. A gesture of comfort. Reassurance.

But then she thought better of it. Thought the move might be too forward at this particular moment. Too much of an intrusion.

"My world changed after Jennifer was born. I was young and pretty irresponsible, but there's something about holding a baby in your arms—a baby *you* helped create—that turns you on your head and sobers you up pretty fast. As soon as I saw that beautiful little face, I knew I had to do something with my life. Make a decent home for her.

"A little over three years later, I graduated from law school and accepted a position with a firm in New Mexico. We hadn't been there two months when Becky and Jen were coming home from swim class and stopped at the corner grocery store for some milk."

He paused again, and in that brief silence, Tara felt her heart breaking. She knew what was coming and wasn't sure now that she wanted to hear it.

"They were at the checkout counter when a couple of hopped-up street punks came in and started waving guns around. Cleaned out all the cash registers. Nobody really knows why they started shooting, but by the time they were done…" He paused. "I was at the office working late when my cell phone rang. I'll never forget that call."

He again lapsed into silence and Tara could imagine him running that phone call through his head. Could even imagine her own father making it.

Mr. Hathaway?

Yes?

This is Sergeant Ed Richmond. Are you the husband of Rebecca Hathaway?

Tara felt tears coming on and closed her eyes, shutting the thought out of her mind.

Then Matt said, "You want to know the irony of it all?"

"What?"

"After everything was said and done, I went home that night, didn't really know what to do with myself. Kept feeling as if Becky and Jen would walk in the door at any moment, even though I'd identified their bodies only two hours before. I don't know why I went to the refrigerator, I wasn't hungry. But right there on the top shelf was a carton of milk, still half-full. Enough to last at least another day. Turned out they didn't really need to stop at the store at all...."

Tara felt heartsick. Could imagine Matt standing at that open refrigerator, staring at that carton of milk, the *if-only*s running through his head.

She'd had a lifetime of *if-only*s and knew that fate could sometimes be very cruel.

But she'd never experienced this kind of cruelty.

"It took me a while to get myself together," Matt said. "I quit the law firm, thought about moving to Europe or South America, anywhere that put some distance between me and that terrible night. I wasn't very pleasant to be around, but a friend of mine in the bureau convinced me to channel my pain into putting scum like those two street punks in jail. Next thing I knew I was training at Quantico. And now, for better or worse, here we are."

She could feel him looking at her now. Could feel those piercing green-gray eyes studying her in the darkness, seeing nothing but shadows and the sliver of moonlight that played along the edges of her face. Her own eyes were filled with tears and she wondered if he saw them, too.

"That's why I had to tell you who I was," he said. "Back at the cabin. I couldn't stand there and watch you go through what Becky and Jen…"

He didn't finish again, and she thought he might be choking back a few tears of his own.

Tara didn't hesitate this time.

Reaching out, she found his hand and squeezed it, and at that moment, her attraction to him was a living, palpable thing.

It was beyond her control now. That incessant naysayer who always seemed to be perched on her shoulder could take a long vacation as far as she was concerned.

She could stop and reevaluate later, couldn't she? Save the rational decisions for a more rational time. Wait until they were both a little less vulnerable, a little less scared. Until the light of day sobered them, brought them to their senses.

But right now the darkness was calling and all she wanted to do was touch him.

Matt didn't seem to mind.

He brought his free hand up, once again stroking her face. "I wasn't dreaming, was I? The angel I saw. That was you."

Then his hand moved to the back of her neck, gently urging her forward. She felt the heat from his body as he leaned toward her in the darkness, and it took everything she had to contain herself, the anticipation of his kiss almost too much to bear.

And just as their lips were about to brush—

The door of the shack burst open, and the beam of a flashlight shone directly in their faces.

Tara heard the ratchet of a shotgun as a woman's voice said, "Who in hades are you, and what're you doing in my house?"

Chapter Ten

"Come on, get up. On your feet. Both of you."

The slight quaver to the woman's voice gave away her age. Even with the flashlight beam blinding them, Tara guessed that she was getting up there in years.

"I've got triple-ought buck in this scattergun, so I'll only tell you one more time. On. Your. Feet."

Tara could feel Matt tensing beside her as they did as they were told, rising slowly, their hands in the air. He stepped forward slightly and shielded Tara with his body.

"There's no need for the weapon," he said, squinting against the light. "We're not a threat to you."

"You're just tourists, is that it?"

"Something like that."

"You break into my home and you think I should just smile and say, 'Have a nice day'?"

Tara gestured with her hands, trying to calm the woman down. "I don't blame you for being upset, but we're in trouble and—"

"Oh, I can see that. You both look like you been rode hard and put away wet. But that don't mean you got a right to trespass."

"Look," Matt said. "We're sorry. We thought the place was abandoned."

"I guess you thought wrong then, didn't you?"

"Ma'am, let's not make this any worse than it has to be. I'm Special Agent Matt Hathaway. I'm with the FBI. And right now you're impeding an investigation."

"FBI? You expect me to believe that?"

"It's the truth."

The flashlight beam swept over Matt's body, then returned to his eyes. He squinted again.

"You gotta be the sorriest federal agent I've ever laid eyes on," the woman said. "Unless running around without a shirt is part of the uniform these days. And it seems to me the only investigation going on here is the two of you getting ready to investigate each other's body parts."

Tara felt herself redden.

"I know this looks bad," Matt said, "but I can explain. So why don't you put the weapon down and let's talk this over."

"Mister, if you think I give two hoots about what some lying son of a..." She didn't finish the sentence and stayed silent for a moment. "Why do you look familiar to me? Have we met before?"

"I can't see your face, but don't think so, no."

"Wait a minute, wait a minute. I saw you on the TV this afternoon. You're one of them boys who escaped from—"

Without thinking, Tara launched herself forward and grabbed for the shotgun. It was a crazy, impulsive move—not her first of the day—and she heard Matt shout a warning behind her, but it was too late. Then the old woman was shouting, too, as Tara's hands wrapped around the barrel and shoved it upward.

The flashlight tumbled to the floor, and the two started struggling, playing tug-of-war over the weapon.

Then Matt was there, wrenching it away from them. "All right, that's it! Everybody calm down."

It was only then that Tara realized that both she and the old woman had sunk to their knees. The woman stopped struggling and Tara released her.

Matt ratcheted the action on the shotgun, over and over, unloading it, letting the shells drop to the floor. Then he picked up the flashlight and shone it in Tara's face.

"What's the matter with you?" he said, sounding like a cop for the first time since she'd met him. It was a sound so familiar to her that she could almost see her father glaring at her from behind that light. "You could've gotten us both killed."

"I'm sorry," she said, blurting it out like a chastened

child. She felt as if she'd been transported through some kind of time warp to a previous decade. "I… I just reacted."

The old woman stirred next to her, her voice quavering worse than ever. "What are you gonna do to me?"

Matt put the light on her, exposing her face for the first time, which was deeply tanned and noticeably weathered. She was edging toward her late seventies, and despite the weathering, she looked frail and wide-eyed and was obviously scared out of her wits.

Which, of course, made Tara feel even worse.

She had just beaten up on a grandmother.

"Relax, ma'am," Matt said. "No one's going to hurt you."

Still stung by his scolding, Tara reached out and helped the old woman to her feet.

"I have an idea," Tara said. "Why don't we all start over?"

HER NAME WAS IMOGENE, and she'd been exaggerating slightly when she said she lived here.

The truth was, her family had owned the place for several decades, and Imogene came up here once in a while to get away from her good-for-nothing son.

They had hoped she was carrying a cell phone, but she told them she wouldn't own one if her life depended on it.

"The world managed to function just fine before everybody and his brother had a phone plastered to his ear. That's all you see anymore. That and a bunch of teenagers sending silly messages to each other. It's enough to drive you crazy."

As Imogene spoke, Tara fired up the lamp again so they could all see. She had been worried that the light might attract unwanted eyes, but Imogene assured her that it wouldn't be anything unusual, and the chances of being noticed were pretty slim.

"Nobody comes around here," she said. "Hell, hardly anyone even knows this place exists. And that's just the way I like it."

"The question is," Matt said, "how did *you* get here? Do you live nearby?"

He had put his battered shirt back on, but left it unbuttoned.

"How you think I got here? I drove."

Tara was surprised. "We didn't hear a car pull in."

Imogene smiled. "The way you two looked, I probably could've pulled a bulldozer into that yard and you wouldn't have noticed."

Tara felt herself redden again as Matt went to the window, looking outside. "So where is it?"

"Look, son, you may have me over a barrel, but if you think I'm gonna aid and abet a fugitive from justice..."

"I told you, I'm with the FBI."

She snorted. "You got a badge or something to back that up?"

"You'll just have to trust me. If you don't, a lot of people could die tomorrow."

Imogene frowned. "What's that supposed to mean? Is that some kind of threat?"

Tara could see that Matt was getting agitated. This old woman was their only hope of reaching civilization before The Brotherhood put their plan into action, and he was obviously more concerned with saving lives right now than wasting time explaining himself or sparing anyone's delicate sensibilities.

Tara thought the appearance of Imogene had probably reminded him of who he was and what he did for a living, and he was suddenly all business.

"I'm not threatening anyone," Matt said, clearly struggling to keep his voice level. "But there are some men not too far from here who are. They're planning to do some very nasty things tomorrow morning, and unless I can get to the city, a lot of innocent lives will be lost. So give me the keys to your car and point me to it."

"Son," Imogene said, "you wanna tell me why I should believe a word you just said, when everyone on the TV is saying you're a fugitive from justice?"

"Because I've been working undercover. The two

men who escaped with me are Carl Maddox and Rusty Zane. Part of a group called The Brotherhood."

Imogene's face screwed up in surprise. "Zane? One of them boys is a Zane?"

"You know them?" Tara asked.

"Family's been living in these parts for half a century. Never did like 'em much. And if you're messed up with that bunch of boneheads you're either crazy as an outhouse rat, or you're telling me the truth."

"Then you'll help us?"

"Don't see as how I have much of a choice," Imogene said. "But tell me. This nasty thing they're about to do. What exactly is it?"

"They're planning to blow up the Whitestone federal courthouse."

Imogene frowned. "You sure about that?"

"Stood right in the room while they were planning it."

Imogene shifted her gaze to Tara, and Tara nodded. "I heard it, too."

"Well, then, what the heck are we waiting for?" She dug into her pocket and tossed a set of car keys to Matt. "Hope you can drive a stick."

Matt smiled at her. "I'll manage."

But before they could move, they heard the sudden thunder of horses' hooves, and Matt quickly gestured them away from the window.

Carl and his crew rode into the yard and came to a sudden stop, their horses huffing and braying.

They were silent for a moment, and Tara chanced a peek outside, saw Carl and the others carrying shotguns with flashlight mounts, their faces set with cold, hard determination. A look that said they'd get what they wanted no matter what it took.

Carl sniffed the air, his pockmarked face spreading into that now familiar grin as he swept his flashlight across the yard and settled its beam on the shack window.

"If I ain't mistaken, boys, I believe we've just found ourselves a couple of grade-A, government-franchised rodents."

Chapter Eleven

Matt grabbed Tara's arm and pulled her away from the window.

His first instinct was to douse the lamp, but then he realized there wasn't much point. He should never have let Tara turn it back on, and Carl already knew someone was inside the shack.

Outside, Maddox was in his usual form. "Hey, hey, Nicky boy, let's make this easy. You come out without a fuss, and you have my word we won't hurt the reporter lady."

His word?

Matt almost laughed.

Maybe they'd apologize for the inconvenience and give Tara a ride into the city, too.

How gullible did Carl think he was?

"What is this?" Imogene whispered. "Some kind of posse?"

"More like a lynch mob," Matt told her, then

quickly surveyed the shack. "I don't suppose there's a back way out of here?"

"Sure," she said, gesturing toward a dark corner. "Just head down that hallway, out past the kitchen, and on through the family room."

Matt frowned at her. "A simple 'no' would've worked."

"You got eyes, don't you? Don't waste my time with stupid questions. I take it these are Zane's men? The ones you claim are planning to blow up the courthouse?"

"It's not a claim," Tara said. "We told you that."

"Either way, it looks like they're getting ready to blow us up, and I may be old, but I like being in one piece."

"You hear me, Nick?" Carl shouted. "No reason this has to get any uglier. I don't care about the girl. I just want you."

Matt held up the keys. "Where's this car of yours?"

"With those lunkheads on the loose, just far enough away to make getting to it an iffy proposition."

Of course, Matt thought.

Why should it be easy?

But then he'd spent the past several hours—not to mention the past seven years—battling bad breaks, and he'd managed to survive so far.

No reason that should change now.

But it wasn't his own survival that worried him. There was Tara to think about, and now Imogene, and potentially hundreds of others.

There was only one way out of this.

"How fast can you move?"

"Depends on the motivation," Imogene said. "But I figure I can hold my own. Why?"

He handed Tara her car keys. "Here's how this is going to work."

Tara's eyes widened. "What are you planning?"

"Just listen," he said. "I'm going to do my best to distract these guys, and when I do, I want you and Imogene to get to that car, as fast as humanly possible."

Tara shook her head. "They'll kill you. They'll kill all of us."

He grabbed the shells off the floor and started reloading the shotgun. "I won't let that happen. And we can't just sit here and hope they'll go away. What's important is that you get to a phone and contact the police, tell them what Zane's up to."

"Like they'll believe me."

"*Make* them believe you. Tell them to get hold of Agent Abernathy or Everhardt with the Anti-Terrorist Task Force. They'll confirm who I am and what my assignment was."

"Are you sure you can trust them? Didn't Zane say he had a mole in the bureau?"

Frank Everhardt had recruited Matt for the mission, and Lloyd Abernathy had been his direct contact. Both men knew about his past, and as much as it killed him to think this, either of them could easily be Zane's informant.

But which one?

Everhardt was a veteran agent with a long, decorated history in law enforcement, while Abernathy was a cocky young upstart who sometimes played fast and loose with the rules.

But none of this told Matt who the mole might be.

"Everhardt," he said finally, relying purely on instinct. "Tell them to contact Everhardt."

Tara shook her head again and grabbed his forearm. "*You* tell them. I'm not going without you."

He pried her fingers away. "You don't have a choice."

He handed the flashlight to Imogene, then grabbed the lantern and crossed the room. Running a hand along the rear wall, he checked for weak spots in the wood.

"How old is this place?"

"You really have to ask?" Imogene said.

He gave her a look, then found what he was hoping for and pressed against it, feeling the wood give slightly. A couple good kicks would do the trick.

"All right," he told them, "I'm going to make a

hole, and it won't be quiet. As soon as Carl and his boys hear wood splintering, they'll come running. So I need you two to get your butts out of here pronto."

"Matt, please, this is crazy."

"Can you think of a better plan?"

Tara stared at him, on the verge of tears. Then she shook her head, and he could tell by her look that she knew he was right.

He just hoped this wasn't the last time he'd see that beautiful face.

Carl was shouting again. "I'm losing my patience, Nicky. You got to the count of three to come out on your own, or we come in, guns blazing."

Matt looked at Imogene. "Which way is the car from here?"

She gestured. "Up the hill, through the mine."

"Through the *mine?*"

"One!" Carl shouted.

Imogene frowned. "Is that a problem for you, Mr. FBI? I keep it parked on the other side of the mountain. The mine takes you straight to it, more or less."

"All right, fine," Matt said, then pumped the shotgun, jacking a round into the chamber. "Let's do it."

"Two!"

Carl was obviously having fun with this, when the

smart thing to do would be to forgo the counting and strike.

But then Carl wasn't exactly smart, was he?

Matt gestured for them to come in closer, then brought his foot up.

He waited a moment, and when Carl shouted, "Three!" Matt jammed a heel into the wall, feeling it give without much resistance, the wood groaning and splintering.

He kicked again, breaking through this time. Then, using the butt of the shotgun, he hammered at the splintered wood, opening up a hole in the wall, just big enough for Tara and Imogene to squeeze through.

"Go! Go!" he shouted, and as the two swept past him, Tara's eyes met his, a look that said, "Be safe," as her fingers grazed his arm.

And then they were outside and Matt moved to the window just in time to see Carl and his men quickly dismounting their horses, three of them heading straight for the shack as three more fanned out to surround it.

Matt didn't hesitate. He fired the shotgun, aiming high, sending a round into the air.

Carl and his men ducked, dropping into a crouch. They began firing back, and Matt fell away from the window as bullets gouged the walls and floor around him.

When the barrage passed, he jumped up, fired

off two more rounds—taking down one of them—then went into a dive and rolled behind the stove for cover.

More bullets gouged the wood around him, clanged against the stove. He knew he was outgunned; there was no way he'd survive this onslaught. He just hoped he had held them off long enough for Tara and Imogene to reach the mine.

Now it was time to get his own butt up there.

Jumping to his feet, he tucked the shotgun under his arm and ran for the hole in the wall—which had been fine for the two women, but was barely large enough for him to squeeze through. Ducking low, he pushed forward, wood scraping against his wound as he went, hot pain blossoming in his bicep.

But he didn't slow down.

Then he was outside, in near pitch darkness, turning toward the direction of the mine—when a flashlight beam washed across his back and someone shouted, "Freeze!"

Matt didn't hesitate.

Dropping to the ground, he went into a roll and turned, bringing up the shotgun. A muzzle flashed and he fired back, the roar of the blast hammering his eardrums as the flashlight went down.

Then he was on his feet again, trying to get his bearings, as he stumbled through the darkness, hustling past two more shacks before he reached an incline and started up the mountain.

Moving through the trees, he heard more shouts echoing behind him.

"There he is! He's headed for the mine!"

Matt picked up speed and saw Tara and Imogene at the top of the incline as Imogene pulled a loose sheet of plywood away from a hole in the side of the mountain and guided Tara inside with the flashlight.

Suddenly, bullets gouged the dirt around them and Tara screamed, diving for cover.

Matt spun around and pumped the shotgun, firing into the trees. Once, twice, three times.

Then nothing. The shotgun was empty.

Behind him, Tara shouted, "Hurry, Matt, hurry!" and he didn't argue, thinking this was probably some very sound advice.

Ditching the weapon, he scrambled up the trail toward her voice.

TARA'S HEART POUNDED wildly as she crouched at the mine entrance, watching Matt run up the hill, bullets now scattering the dirt around him.

Below, flashlight beams crisscrossed through the trees like tiny searchlights as Zane's men made their way up the hill after him, guns flashing.

Then suddenly Matt grunted and fell, and Tara felt her chest seize up—

Oh my God, oh my God.

But a second later he was on his feet again, seemingly unharmed, zigzagging wildly, making himself as difficult a target as possible.

Bullets continued to zing past him, and Tara knew it was a miracle that he hadn't been hit again. But Carl's men were shooting in the dark and on the run, which made it difficult enough to hit a *stationary* target.

Then Matt was inside the mine, grabbing her sleeve and pulling her along, shouting, "Go! Go!" as, up ahead, Imogene waved her flashlight, signaling for them to follow.

The mine was a maze of narrow tunnels, reinforced by centuries-old lumber, and Tara knew that without a guide, they could easily get lost in here.

They quickly worked their way up a short incline toward Imogene.

When they reached her, the old woman took one look at Matt, said, "You're a crazy son of a gun, aren't you?" then hurried them through the shaft.

They were several yards in when flashlight beams appeared at the mouth of the tunnel. Urgent and angry voices echoed through the mine, Carl's the loudest of them all.

"You should've cooperated, Nick. Now we're gonna have to get nasty. You ready for some fun, cutie-pie?"

Tara felt her chest tighten again, wishing she could just close her eyes and will these people away.

When would it be over?

"I gotta give those boys credit," Imogene murmured. "They don't give up easy."

No they don't, Tara thought.

But neither do we.

"Faster," Matt said. "We gotta move faster."

Feeling his hand on her back, urging her forward, Tara followed Imogene's lead as the old woman picked up speed and veered to the right. But now Carl and his men were running, closing in behind them.

"How much farther?" Matt asked.

Imogene gestured with the flashlight. "Just around this bend and we'll be home free."

It occurred to Tara that while they may well reach Imogene's car, that didn't guarantee they'd be able to get inside, get it started and pull away before their pursuers opened fire. And at the moment, *home free* sounded more like a pipe dream than a reality.

Her fears were confirmed when they reached the end of the tunnel, only to find themselves at a three-way junction, two more shafts branching off to the left and the right. Imogene came to a sudden stop and turned around, facing the direction they'd just come from, as if waiting for Carl and his men to get closer.

Matt and Tara almost collided with her.

"What are you doing?" Matt said. "We have to keep moving."

"Watch and see," Imogene told him.

Smiling now, she stepped to the side of the tunnel where a frayed section of rope that hung from the ceiling was tied to one of the wooden braces. She quickly untied it, then pointed her flashlight beam down the tunnel as Carl and crew came into view.

They were several yards away when Carl held up a hand, bringing his men to a halt, another grin spreading across his pockmarked face.

"What's this?" he said, squinting against the light. "You're giving up so easily? Looks like I overestimated you, Nick."

They brought their guns up.

"Careful, boys. Don't shoot the reporter. She and I have some unfinished—"

Imogene yanked on the rope and, down the shaft, a brace broke away and the ceiling caved in, letting loose an avalanche of dirt, rock and debris, forcing Carl and his men to stumble back to avoid getting hit.

A moment later, the ground they had occupied was replaced by a wall of fallen rock.

Tara and Matt stared at it incredulously as Imogene's smile widened.

"Safety precaution," she said. "You never know who you might run into up here."

Chapter Twelve

Several minutes later, they emerged from the mine
on the opposite side of the mountain.

An old Rambler station wagon that looked as
if it hadn't been washed for a decade, or seen any
bodywork in at least two, was parked at the side of
a road that wound downward through the trees into
darkness.

Far below, the lights of the city twinkled, and Tara
thought it might be the most beautiful sight she'd ever
seen. But then anything would look beautiful right
now. She was relieved and exhausted and just wanted
to get back to Whitestone.

As Imogene made her way to the Rambler, Tara and
Matt stood back a moment, taking in those lights.

"So many people," Matt said, a faraway look in
his eyes. "They work their jobs, go home to their
families, have dinner together, watch TV. And they
never know when tragedy can strike. When someone
like Zane and that maniac Carl can come crashing

down on them, destroying everything they know and love."

Tara felt a sudden hitch in her throat as she thought about grocery stores and cartons of milk and drugged-out punks and mothers and daughters who go out on an errand and never come home again.

She looked at Matt. "Not this time," she said. "Thanks to you."

"It isn't over yet."

"It will be. And I've got a mother, a sister and a couple of nieces who'll be thanking you, too."

"Maybe they should be thanking Imogene," Matt said. "If it weren't for her little booby trap, we'd probably be facedown in that mine right now."

As if on cue, the Rambler's horn honked.

"I can't start this jalopy without the keys," Imogene called out. "You two lovebirds want to hurry it up?"

THEY RODE IN SILENCE, Tara up front with Imogene as Matt stretched his hard frame across the backseat and quietly dozed.

Tara felt drained, as if some invisible plug had been pulled from her body, letting all the energy leak out. She was battered and bruised and figured she must look like something that had just risen from the grave.

Rode hard and put away wet, Imogene had said.

Get **2** Books **FREE!**

Harlequin® Books,
publisher of women's fiction,
presents

HARLEQUIN®

INTRIGUE®

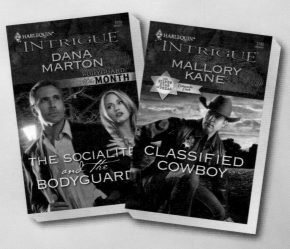

GET 2 BOOKS

We'd like to send you two *Harlequin Intrigue*®
novels absolutely free. Accepting them puts you
under no obligation to purchase any more books.

HOW TO GET YOUR
2 FREE BOOKS AND 2 FREE GIFTS

1. Return the reply card today, and we'll send you two *Harlequin Intrigue* novels, absolutely free! We'll even pay the postage!

2. Accepting free books places you under no obligation to buy anything, ever. Whatever you decide, the free books and gifts are yours to keep, free!

3. We hope that after receiving your free books you'll want to remain a subscriber, but the choice is yours—to continue or cancel, any time at all!

EXTRA BONUS

You'll also get two free mystery gifts! (worth about $10)

FREE!

Return this card promptly to get
2 FREE BOOKS and 2 FREE GIFTS!

 HARLEQUIN®

INTRIGUE®

YES! Please send me 2 FREE *Harlequin Intrigue*®
novels, and 2 free mystery gifts as well. I understand
I am under no obligation to purchase anything, as
explained on the back of this insert.

*About how many NEW paperback fiction books have
you purchased in the past 3 months?*

❑ 0-2	❑ 3-6	❑ 7 or more
EZQ3	EZS3	EZTF

❑ I prefer the regular-print edition   ❑ I prefer the larger-print edition
182/382 HDL   199/399 HDL

FIRST NAME	LAST NAME

ADDRESS

APT.#	CITY

STATE/PROV.	ZIP/POSTAL CODE

Visit us at:
www.ReaderService.com

◀ **DETACH AND MAIL CARD TODAY!** ▶

Tara couldn't think of a description more apt than that one.

After a while, Imogene glanced in her rearview mirror at Matt. "So how long have you and Mr. FBI known each other?"

"What time is it?" Tara asked.

Imogene glanced at her wristwatch. "Closing in on midnight."

"About seven hours, then."

Tara heard herself say the words, but couldn't quite believe them. It seemed as if a century had passed since Carl had grabbed her in Susan's cabin.

Imogene's eyebrows raised. "Seven hours?" she said. "You two work fast."

"What do you mean?"

"When I walked in on you, dearie, you looked as if you were about ready to jump his bones."

Tara tried to protest, but Imogene bulldozed her way past it.

"Not that I blame you. He's a helluva specimen. And that torn-up shirt doesn't hurt the image, either. Makes you want to tear up the pants, too."

Tara felt herself redden again. She wasn't particularly prone to blushing, but hearing this old woman say what she herself had been thinking half the night was embarrassing the heck out of her.

She turned, making sure that Matt was asleep.

"It's not like that," she said. "He's a cop. And I have no interest in cops."

Imogene looked at her. "You actually fool yourself with a line like that?"

"I'm not trying to fool anyone."

"Uh-huh," the old woman said. "One thing I've learned in all my years on this Earth is this. You're presented with an opportunity, you'd better take it, because you might not get the chance again. And, child, I've seen the way that boy looks at you. That's the kind of look that only comes around once in a lifetime."

Tara felt her heart skip slightly, but pushed the feeling away.

"What about you?" Tara asked. "You ever meet Mr. Right?"

Imogene snorted. "What I met was Mr. Wrong, who up and left me right before Mr. Wrong, Jr. was born. Takes everything I got to keep that kid on track, but he's finally coming around."

"Oh? What does he do?"

"For a living? He's in construction. You know that new Performing Arts Center? That's one of the sites he worked on."

Tara nodded. "My station has been covering it. And I'm supposed to be at the dedication ceremony tomorrow."

"You're a reporter, right? I thought I heard one of those idiots back in the mine call you that."

Tara shook her head. "A segment producer."

"And what exactly does that mean?"

"I look for story ideas, listen to pitches from reporters, arrange interviews, stuff like that. It's not very glamorous, but I enjoy it."

"You ever meet any movie stars?"

Tara laughed. "Whitestone isn't exactly a hot spot for the Hollywood crowd. But, who knows, there may be a few at the dedication tomorrow. Along with the mayor, the governor and a handful of big business types. You should stop by. You may get lucky and see somebody famous."

Imogene nodded. "I might just do that," she said, and gave Tara a wink.

THE DRIVE SEEMED TO take forever.

Halfway down the mountain, Tara felt herself starting to nod off. She resisted at first—some kind of survival mechanism kicking in—then finally succumbed to the temptation and let her mind drift away.

A moment later she was dreaming, images flickering through her brain, speeding up, slowing down, flashing intermittently like gunshots in the dark.

A crying child.

An empty classroom.

A stern-faced teacher checking her watch.

Then, without warning, Tara was back in the mine, crouching next to one of the dilapidated wooden braces, looking in horror at the pile of rock and debris left by Imogene's booby trap as it began to rumble and shift.

"He's coming through," Imogene said, and it was only then that Tara realized that the old woman was crouched next to her.

But when Tara turned to face her, she didn't see Imogene at all.

It was her mother.

Wearing a wedding dress.

Her mother nodded toward the pile of rock as it continued to shift. Several chunks of debris fell away, leaving behind a jagged hole in the wall.

"He made it," she said. "He's here."

"Who? Who is it?"

"Who do you think?"

Then a face appeared behind the wall—the hard, cold-eyed face of Ed Richmond, one of Whitestone's finest. Career cop, cheating husband, absentee father.

Tara's absentee father.

But the moment their gazes met, he was gone in a flash of bright white light, and Tara turned around to find herself standing in a funeral home, an open coffin only feet away from her.

A woman sat nearby, dressed in black, tears in her eyes, and Tara recognized her immediately.

Lila Sinclair. *Detective* Lila Sinclair, to be more precise. Her father's ex-partner, second wife and now widow. This was the very same woman who had sat at the family table for Thanksgiving dinner when Tara was sixteen. The woman who had shared a motel room with Detective Richmond the night a burglar broke into his home and tried to rape his wife.

Tears streamed down Lila's cheeks, but Tara averted her gaze, not wanting to see that face, not wanting to talk to her, despising her simply for who she was and what she represented.

Instead, Tara turned her attention to the open coffin and slowly strode toward it, feeling as if she were moving through a vat of molasses, each step an effort, her heart in her throat as she drew closer and closer.

Grief gripped her as she came to a stop and stared down at the body inside. Eyes closed. Arms crossed over his chest.

But to her surprise, it wasn't her father.

It was Matt.

TARA JERKED AWAKE, sucking in a breath, and swiveled her head toward the backseat. Matt was still stretched across it, fast asleep, his bare chest rising and falling rhythmically.

Uneasiness quaked through her and settled in her stomach, the image of him lying in that coffin lingering in her mind's eye, an uninvited ghost. She shook it away, and hugged herself as if to ward off a chill.

"You okay, hon?"

Imogene. Keeping her gaze on the road.

"Bad dream," Tara said.

"Boy, do I know *that* territory. But I sleep like a baby, now."

"Oh? How do you manage that?"

"I don't let things build up inside. Something bothers me, I take action, do something about it." She looked at Tara. "Sometimes you just gotta shake things up, you know? Throw off your chains and air your grievances. Find a way to turn a bad dream into a good one."

Tara was tempted to point out to Imogene that she had just spouted about every pop psychology cliché that Tara had ever heard, but she bit her tongue. The old woman was only trying to make her feel better.

But Tara *didn't* feel better. The sense of unease the dream had given her had not yet dissipated, and she had to wonder if her unconscious mind had been trying to tell her something.

Or confirm what she already knew.

That getting involved with Special Agent Matt Hathaway would be nothing but heartache.

Chapter Thirteen

It was past midnight when they reached the city.

Whitestone was a sprawling mix of urban sophistication and western charm, home to old families with long histories. But with the sudden influx of new residents over the past decade, it had begun to rebuild and reinvent itself, a process that was slowly destroying what made the place unique.

Now, strip malls, fast food drive-throughs and cookie-cutter apartment complexes dominated the neighborhoods, and Tara had a feeling that anyone visiting from, say, Los Angeles or Phoenix would feel as if they'd never left home.

As they pulled onto the main highway, Imogene pointed toward the outbound lanes.

Flashing blue lights ahead.

Highway patrol cars.

Glowing road flares blocked off all but one of the oncoming lanes, causing a line of traffic at least a quarter of a mile long.

Even the traffic on *their* side of the highway had slowed to a crawl.

It may have been a Friday night, but Tara didn't think this was a drunk-driving checkpoint.

Imogene smirked as they drew closer to it. "Looks like the little blue bears are having a hissy fit over your new boyfriend."

Surprised by her tone, Tara eyed her reproachfully.

"What?" the old woman said. "You think you're the only one who has a problem with cops? Just 'cause I'm pushin' eighty don't mean I'm Mother Teresa. Too many of these boys got a sense of entitlement that truly chaps my butt."

Tara said nothing. God knew she had her own prejudices, but she definitely didn't share Imogene's sentiments. Her father may have had his problems, but a sense of entitlement had not been one of them. And she certainly hadn't seen it in Matt.

He was stirring now, coming awake, and she wondered if he had heard Imogene.

She glanced at the activity across the highway, then reached over and put a hand on his shoulder.

"Stay down," she said softly.

He did as he was told, keeping his head low as they rolled past the road block. Fortunately, CSHP wasn't checking the inbound cars.

"We need to find a phone," he said.

Tara gestured to the patrol cars. "Or we could flag these guys down and tell them what's happening."

"And spend the next two days wading through their territorial baloney? No thanks. They probably would have listened to you, but once they see a wanted fugitive, the game is over. I have to get hold of Everhardt."

Tara nodded, suddenly realizing that now that they were clear of danger, she not only wanted to divert a disaster, but was just as anxious to bring down The Brotherhood as Matt was. The shock of the past several hours was starting to wear off, and she could feel anger quickly replacing it.

Those creeps had almost killed her.

She wasn't sure what had triggered this feeling. Imogene's comment about the little blue bears, maybe. Not so much the words, but the way in which they'd been spoken. The not-so-subtle hint of scorn beneath them.

It had reminded her of Carl and Rusty and Jimmy Zane. And any thoughts involving them were bound to make her angry. Especially Carl.

She could still feel his paw squeezing her breast, and a shudder of revulsion ran through her.

She turned to Imogene.

"Phone," she echoed. "Let's find a phone."

THERE WAS AN EZ-MART on Charleston, just east of the highway. Imogene pulled the Rambler into the lot and parked away from the bright fluorescent lights of the storefront.

The phone kiosk next to the entrance was graffiti-scarred and battered, but it looked functional.

Matt pulled himself upright and opened his door. His joints were stiff from lack of use and he couldn't wait to get out of this car.

He looked at Imogene. "You mind taking Tara home?"

Tara turned sharply. "What are you talking about?"

"I've put you through enough," he said. "You need to go home and get some rest. I'll handle it from here."

"As much as I'd love to take a nice hot shower and count all my cuts and bruises, I think I'll stick around for a while."

"Why?"

She seemed surprised and even hurt by the question, as if he'd just told her this had been nothing more than a one-night stand. He immediately felt like a fool, and Imogene didn't hesitate to reinforce that feeling.

"Boy, you're as dumb as rocks, aren't you?"

"I didn't mean that the way it sounded," he said to Tara. "But if I call Everhardt and he turns out to be the wrong guy, I don't want you caught in the blowback."

"I've held my own so far, haven't I?"

"That's not the point. You've been lucky. We've both been lucky. And if you were to get hurt now, I'd never forgive myself."

The defiance in her eyes made her even more beautiful. "I'm a grown-up, Matt. I can tie my own shoes and everything."

"I know that, but—"

"And to be honest, this is the biggest story I've ever been involved with. I can't walk away from it now."

Despite himself, Matt felt his heart lift. That Tara wanted to see this through, no matter what the reason, made her all the more attractive to him.

She was, he realized, the first women he'd met since Becky died who possessed the kind of qualities that made him wonder if it was possible to fall in love again.

A boldness of spirit.

A quick, decisive mind.

A face and body which only confirmed that God was a master craftsman.

As much as he might try, he couldn't forget her hands touching him, tending to him, caring for him.

Or that almost-kiss back in Imogene's shack.

And while he knew it was wholly inappropriate to be thinking this right now, he wouldn't mind putting the night on pause and taking a moment to help her count those cuts and bruises.

Still, he'd meant what he said. He wouldn't know what to do with himself if she were to get hurt under his watch.

Under *anyone's* watch.

He was about to tell her this again when she cut him off.

"Look," she said. "This isn't a negotiation. So go make your phone call. I'll be inside, looking for a restroom. If I can't take that shower, at least I can freshen up." She smiled. "I want to look my best when we take down the bad guys."

Matt shook his head and found himself returning the smile.

How could he possibly argue with that?

IT WASN'T UNTIL SHE GOT inside and smelled popcorn and roasting hot dogs that Tara realized she was starving. Her purse and wallet were still laying on the floor of Susan's cabin, however, and she wasn't about to ask Imogene for charity.

The old woman had done far more than anyone could ask of a stranger. Especially under these circumstances. And it was obvious that Imogene wasn't exactly rich. She barely had enough change for Matt to use the pay phone.

He was out there now, standing at the kiosk in

a wrinkled Marine-green T-shirt that Imogene had found in the Rambler's trunk. One of her son's old shirts that read NEVER SURRENDER.

It was a little snug on Matt—which wasn't necessarily a bad thing—but it was considerably less conspicuous than a torn and bloody prison shirt.

Tara wished she had a change of clothes, too. Her V-neck was filthy, and when she'd asked the clerk for the restroom key, she was afraid he'd insist that she buy something before handing it over.

But he didn't, and when she got a look at herself in the restroom mirror, she considered this a minor miracle. There was a bruise developing on her right cheekbone, and she had no idea how she'd gotten it. The dirt on her face made it hard to see, but there was no disguising it. She looked like a battered wife.

Tara dabbed at the bruise, felt a small pulse of pain. She let the water run hot, then stripped off her shirt and bra and got to work, washing the grime and sweat and blood off her face, hands, arms and torso, thinking how glorious it was to be clean.

Or, at least, semi-clean.

Discarding the bra, which was too disgusting to deal with, she used damp paper towels to wipe the V-neck, then slipped it back on, following up with a spot check.

Not perfect, but better.

There wasn't much she could do about her hair

but run her fingers through it in hopes of making herself just a little more presentable. Unfortunately, the bruise was still a problem and she wished she had some cover-up.

Ron the Newscaster had once said she was pretty enough to be an on-air anchor, but he would undoubtedly reconsider that opinion if he could see her now.

Thinking this was about as good as it was going to get, Tara grabbed the key off the back of the toilet and exited the restroom.

As she passed through an aisle filled with bags of chips and beef jerky and boxed doughnuts—reminded once again how hungry she was—she looked through the front glass at Matt. He hung up the phone, retrieved some coins from the hopper and fed them back into the slot before dialing another number.

For a moment, their eyes met, Matt frowning at the sight of the bruise. Then his gaze lowered slightly, and Tara remembered that she was no longer wearing a bra. She knew what the friction of the cloth and the cold must be doing to her.

Always the gentleman, however, Matt quickly looked away and went back to his phone call.

It was only then that Tara shifted her attention to the parking lot and felt her chest tighten in alarm. A Whitestone Sheriff's patrol car had just pulled into the empty slot directly behind Matt.

Two young deputies emerged, taking in the stranger at the pay phone kiosk with cold, hard eyes.

MATT STIFFENED when he saw the reflection in the convenience store window: a Sheriff's cruiser, two deputies emerging, giving him the cop stare.

He kept his back to them, his head down, as he pretended to talk on the phone.

The line rang unanswered in his ear.

Was this a hot dog and soda break? Or had these two been notified by the clerk that a wanted fugitive was standing right outside his store?

Matt knew his face was all over the news, and chances were pretty good that there was a television playing quietly behind the counter. But the clerk had barely glanced at him when he and Tara arrived. Spent most of his time ogling Tara as she asked for the restroom key. And if the cops had been called, Matt was pretty sure they'd send in a SWAT team to take him down, not a couple of pavement pounders.

So he told himself that everything was fine, as long as he didn't let them get a look at his face.

He briefly considered Tara's suggestion that they go straight to the cops. Tell these guys who he was and what The Brotherhood was up to. But he knew in his gut that they'd never believe him, and his best bet was to get hold of Everhardt.

Assuming he could get the guy to answer his phone.

The pay phone kiosk was close to the entrance, and Matt could almost feel the heat from the deputies' bodies as they moved past him and stepped inside.

Slowly letting out a breath, he chanced a glance through the glass and saw Tara still standing in the potato chip aisle, clutching the restroom key, which was hooked to a wooden paddle.

She was frozen in place.

Stay calm, he wanted to tell her.

They don't know who you are. Just return the key and come back outside.

Then one of the deputies looked at her, giving her the once-over as he nodded to her in greeting.

Spurred into action, she returned the nod then stepped past him and deposited the key on the counter, thanking the clerk as she turned and headed for the door.

She was almost to it when the deputy said something to her and she turned around.

His gaze went straight to the bruise on her face.

Chapter Fourteen

"You're Tara, right? Tara Richmond?"

Surprised, Tara's pulse quickened.

Did she know this guy?

The deputy must have noticed the confusion in her expression. "We met a few months ago. At your father's funeral." He approached her now, held out a hand to shake. "Jim Wakefield."

Tara hesitated. Her father's funeral had been a bit crazy, crowded with cops of all types, and she hadn't been in the best frame of mind that day. She'd probably seen a hundred different faces and wouldn't be able to pick a single one of them out of a lineup.

"Right," she lied, and quickly shook the hand. "Now I remember."

He stared at her, frowning slightly. She knew he was looking at the bruise.

"You okay? Anything wrong?"

She let out a small laugh. "I'm fine. Why?"

He nodded to her face. "Looks like you had a

run-in with somebody." Then his eyes shifted, looking out the window toward Matt.

Tara could see where he was going and quickly cut him off, gesturing to the bruise with another laugh.

"Oh, this," she said. "I was hiking this afternoon and ran into a tree branch. It looks a lot worse than it feels."

His eyes were still on Matt. "You sure about that?"

Tara hated herself for doing this, but she needed to get this guy's attention away from that window.

"I'm sure," she said. Then, with a subtle shift of her shoulders, she arched her back slightly and thrust her chest forward, just enough to emphasize that she wasn't wearing a bra. The V-neck's fabric was thin enough to make this very apparent. "Why wouldn't I be?"

As she had hoped, the deputy's nipple radar kicked in and he returned his attention to her, first glancing at her breasts, then, reluctantly, at her face again, attempting to be subtle about it and failing miserably.

Men are so predictable sometimes.

"No reason," he said, clearing his throat. "Hazards of the job. You see a bruise like that, you start thinking the worst."

Tara smiled. "I'm just a klutz. Little bit of makeup and it'll hardly be noticeable." She shook his hand again. "It was good seeing you, Jim. And thanks for your concern."

He doffed an imaginary cap and she smiled and turned to go.

"Hey, Tara."

She stopped, her level of discomfort rising with each second she was forced to stand there, knowing that Matt was still in his field of view.

"You work at KWEST News, right?"

"Right," she said.

"You mind if I call you sometime?"

He was on the skinny side, slightly balding, and while he seemed like a nice enough guy, he was not even remotely Tara's type, even excluding the whole cop thing.

But she smiled again anyway. "Sure."

Then she was out the door, moving past Matt and straight to the Rambler and Imogene.

As she climbed in, she glanced back toward the phone kiosk and saw Matt heading toward the street as if they didn't exist.

Inside, Deputy Jim had joined his partner at the soda and hot dog counter, the two exchanging grins, obviously talking about her. She had a feeling she'd be the topic of conversation for the rest of their shift. But she didn't care. The distraction had worked.

And as the two deputies turned their attention to filling their stomachs, Tara let out a sigh of relief.

THEY FOUND MATT about a block down the street. As he threw the door open and climbed into the Rambler's backseat, he said, "Sorry, Imogene. You probably thought you were rid of us."

"Like I've got anything better to do."

"I'll never be able to repay you for this. You're taking a pretty big leap of faith, and I appreciate that."

Imogene dismissed him with a wave of the hand. "You don't get to be as old as I am without taking a risk or two. Where to next?"

"That's a good question," he said, sounding troubled.

Tara turned, studied him. "What is it? What's wrong?"

"I couldn't get through to Everhardt *or* Abernathy. They didn't pick up."

"You've got to be kidding me."

"I wish I were."

"So what does that mean?"

He shook his head. "I'm not sure. They must both know about the prison escape, but only one of them knows that The Brotherhood is on to me—and he undoubtedly thinks I'm dead. The other one probably assumes the operation is going forward as scheduled and has no idea I'm on the run."

"That doesn't explain why they're not answering."

"No kidding," Matt said. "And I still don't know which one to trust. I was hoping a surprise phone call would be enough to tip someone's hand, but now I'll just have to show up in person and hope for the best."

"Everhardt?"

He shrugged. "It's a coin toss at this point. But, yeah, my money's still on him. Let's just hope I'm right." He looked at Imogene. "One last stop and you're off the hook."

She returned the look in her rearview mirror. "So let me repeat," she said. "Where to?"

"Lakewood Village. Cop Country."

And at the sound of those words, Tara's stomach tightened.

LAKEWOOD VILLAGE WAS an upper-middle-class housing tract in the center of the city.

To Whitestone residents it was known as Cop Country, because so many people in law enforcement had homes in the area. As a child, Tara herself had lived in the neighborhood, but moved away shortly before her seventeenth birthday, when her mom and dad had divorced and sold the house.

With Friday-night traffic, it took Imogene a good thirty minutes to get them there, but as they pulled into the neighborhood, Tara couldn't help feeling a kind of claustrophobia closing in on her.

Everhardt's place was only three blocks and two streets over from her old haunting ground, and it carried the same modest single-story floor plan as her childhood home. It sat in the middle of a cul-de-sac— just like hers—and as Imogene pulled the Rambler to the curb out front, Tara felt as if she'd taken a headlong dive straight into the past.

She halfway expected to see her father's ghost standing in the driveway, glaring at her.

The house itself was dark, but that didn't really mean anything. It was past bedtime for a lot of people. Even FBI agents needed their sleep.

Matt opened his door, then leaned over and patted Imogene's shoulder. "You've just helped us save a lot of lives. Thanks again."

"Yes," Tara said. "Thank you."

Imogene leaned toward the glove box and opened it, taking out an old service revolver. She handed it to Matt.

"Just in case. You two be safe."

Matt took it, tucked it into his waistband and nodded. "You might want to stay away from that shack for a while. Carl and his crew can't be too happy with you right now."

Imogene snickered. "I just wish I'd waited until they were *under* that pile of rocks before I let it loose. But don't worry, I'll bunk with my son tonight. He'll want to hear all about my adventures in wonderland."

With another pat on the shoulder, Matt climbed out, then Tara popped her door open, gave Imogene a grateful smile and joined him on the sidewalk.

As THE OLD WOMAN waved and pulled away, Tara and Matt turned their attention to Everhardt's house.

Moving to the top of the drive, they stepped onto a cobblestone walkway identical to the one Tara had taken every day for more than half her life, a hundred different memories now flooding her mind. There were plenty of good times during those years, a lot of laughs inside that house. So why did she always choose to remember the bad ones?

Her conflict over her father was bordering on obsession these days and she knew she had to purge her mind of this self-absorbed nonsense.

It wasn't healthy.

The more she wrestled with it, the more she realized that despite her protests to Matt that she was a grown-up who could take care of herself, deep down she was still just a child, hoping to find that one man in her life who would love her unconditionally. The void her father had left in her was wider and deeper than anyone could ever know.

For God's sake, Tara, get a grip.

There are more important things in this world than your fragile self-esteem.

As they approached the front porch, Matt came to a

sudden stop and held a hand up, stepping protectively in front of her.

"What? What is it?" she asked.

He put a finger to his lips, then nodded to the front door.

Without the porch light on, it was hard to see, and Tara had been too preoccupied to notice before now.

The door was ajar.

Normally, this wouldn't be all that alarming, but with everything they'd gone through over the past few hours, about a million different red flags went up.

Matt took the revolver from his waistband, keeping his voice low. "Stay here."

Tara shook her head. "Let's not start that again. I go where you go."

Matt made a face, but didn't protest. Probably knew by now that it was an argument he wouldn't win.

They listened a moment, hearing no sound of a disturbance, then moved together onto the porch. Matt reached forward and gently pushed the door open.

It creaked faintly, opening onto a familiar-looking foyer. But where Tara's foyer had been bordered by bookshelves, this one held a narrow table with a vase of dying sunflowers and couple of framed photographs atop it.

A man and a woman, smiling for the camera. Everhardt and his wife, no doubt.

Beyond it was a modestly furnished living room with a fireplace in the corner. Couch, two easy chairs. An outdated knotted pile carpet.

No sign of a disturbance, so far. Nothing looked out of place.

Not that this meant anything.

It wasn't until they were standing on the carpet that Tara heard a television playing faintly in another room. A newscast in progress.

She and Matt exchanged a look, then moved to a hallway to their left and saw light flickering in the doorway at the end of the hall.

Her doorway, Tara thought.

Leading to *her* bedroom.

As she fought off a feeling of déjà vu, Matt put himself in front of her again, then brought the pistol up.

They worked their way down the hall and turned into the doorway to find not a bedroom, but a simple study with bookshelves, a small desk, an armchair and a television tuned to *Gilligan's Island.*

And slumped in the armchair, facing the TV, was the man from the photograph in the foyer.

Special Agent Everhardt.

But he wasn't smiling now.

He had a bullet hole in his right temple.

Chapter Fifteen

"Oh my God…"

Tara felt her knees go weak. Despite all the running and shooting and violence she'd been part of, this was the last thing she'd expected to see.

Everhardt sat with his chin to his chest, his right arm dangling over the arm of the chair, nearly touching the floor.

A Glock 9 mm lay on the carpet within his grasp.

Matt felt Everhardt's neck for a pulse.

From the look on his face, he wasn't getting one.

"Still warm," he said. Then his gaze dropped to Everhardt's lap, where the dead man's left hand rested, clutching a touch-screen cell phone.

Matt snatched a pencil out of a cup on the desk, then returned to Everhardt and stabbed the cell phone's display with the eraser end.

Tara's legs were still trembling, but she moved over beside Matt and looked down at the phone.

On the screen was a text message that Everhardt

had typed out but hadn't sent. The intended recipient was someone name Janice.

"His wife?" Tara asked.

Matt nodded somberly. The message on-screen was only two words: *Forgive me.*

"What do you think this is about?" Tara asked. "Why would he do this?"

Matt stared down at the body, a faraway look in his eyes.

"I'm not sure," he said. "I know he and Janice were having problems. And judging by those flowers in the foyer, I'd say she's been gone a few days." He tried to hide it, but she could see that the sight of his dead colleague was just short of devastating for him. "But I'm thinking this doesn't have anything to do with his marriage."

"What then?"

"Maybe I got it wrong. Maybe Abernathy isn't the turncoat. Maybe it was Everhardt."

"And what? His conscience got the better of him?"

"That would be my guess. Frank was always a by-the-book kind of guy. A strong believer in God and Country. If he strayed in a moment of weakness and fell in with The Brotherhood, the guilt might've been too much for him."

"So he kills himself? Why not just pick up the phone and turn them in? Do the right thing?"

Matt stared down at the body again, the faraway look returning to his eyes. "I guess we'll never know the answer to that one."

Then, as if shaking a heavy weight from his shoulders, he moved back to the desk, reaching for the landline atop it.

"Who are you calling? The police?"

"Not likely. I figure I'd better try Abernathy again."

He quickly punched in a number, waited. Tara could hear the line ringing.

After about seven rings, Matt shook his head. "Still no answer." He hit the hook switch, waited for a dial tone, then punched in another number.

"What now?" she asked.

"FBI automated checkpoint. Before I went deep cover, Everhardt gave me a six-digit emergency code, just in case I encountered a situation like this one. I was about to try this at the convenience store when your friend in uniform decided to get curious."

The line rang twice, then was picked up. A recorded voice murmured something into Matt's ear and he said, "Agent Matt Hathaway. Code Blue. One, seven, three, three, two, six."

The voice murmured again, and Matt frowned.

"One, seven, three, three, two, six," he repeated, emphasizing each number.

The voice murmured a third time, and Matt listened, then hung up, his whole face going slack.

Something was seriously amiss.

"What is it?" Tara asked.

"The system didn't recognize my code." He glanced at the body. "Everhardt must have canceled it."

Tara's gut tightened. "Then that means unless you can get hold of Abernathy..."

Matt nodded. "I've been hung out to dry."

Before they could contemplate this turn of events, the squawk of a police radio echoed in the street outside.

They both turned sharply, exchanged a look.

"Neighbor must've spotted us," Matt whispered. "We need to get out of here."

They quickly started down the hallway, stopping at the edge of the living room, where they had a clear view of the foyer and the street beyond.

Outside, two uniformed deputies, flashlights in hand, were exiting their patrol car and about to head up the cobblestone walkway.

Tara felt panic rising.

She knew the layout of the house, and the only other way out of here was through the kitchen in the rear. But there was no way to get to the kitchen without passing through the living room and being seen.

"Window," Matt said, and they stepped back into Everhardt's study, moving past the body.

But the window was painted shut.

Matt flicked the lever and tried to pry it open, but it wouldn't budge, and they didn't have time to mess with it.

Then it struck Tara.

A third way out.

"Follow me," she said.

Moving again to the hallway, she searched the ceiling until she saw a short rope dangling from it.

When they were kids, she and Susan would hide in the attic whenever their parents fought. They had taken some of their dolls and their favorite books up there, and they'd sit on the rafters, playing quietly, trying not to listen to the angry voices below.

Grabbing the rope, Tara yanked hard.

A narrow hinged hatch opened in the ceiling, letting loose a retractable ladder.

They heard footsteps on the porch now. The deputies were about to enter the foyer.

"Hurry," Matt said.

Tara scrambled up the ladder, Matt following close behind her. As they cleared the threshold, she quickly grabbed a handle mounted inside the hatch and pulled. The ladder collapsed and the door swung shut, closing them inside.

Plunging them into darkness.

Tara let loose a barely audible sigh of relief. They'd

made some noise, but she didn't think they'd been heard.

It was cramped up here, much smaller than she remembered, and as they waited in silence, she could feel Matt's chest against her shoulder, rising and falling with each breath. His breathing seemed a bit more labored than it should, and she wondered how his wound was holding up.

The only light came from a small window on the far side of the attic.

Their ticket out.

It would be only a matter of moments before the deputies found Everhardt's body, and once that happened, this place would be crawling with deputies.

It was now or never.

Matt must have been reading her mind. "We'd better get going," he whispered.

They ducked low, moving at a crouch beneath the rafters, Tara wincing every time the wood beneath their shoes creaked as they crossed the attic and reached the window. The neighbor's place was a two-story, and light from the upstairs bedroom was just enough to illuminate this side of Everhardt's house, showing them a small patch of lawn below, bordered by a tangle of rose bushes.

It wasn't much of a jump, but it could be risky. If Everhardt's house was indeed identical to Tara's, there would be a gutter pipe to the left, running from the roof to the ground, just like the one Tara had shimmied down dozens of times as a kid.

The way their luck was going, however, they'd never be able to get that far.

This window was probably painted shut, too.

But when Matt tried the lever, it turned easily, and a moment later he slid the window open, gesturing for Tara to climb out.

She ducked and went through the opening, saw the familiar aluminum gutter pipe to her left. It looked solid enough, but she'd been a scrawny kid and had to wonder if it could handle the weight of a grown-up. The muffins she inhaled with her coffee every morning didn't seem like such a good idea right now.

Grabbing the pipe, she hoisted herself onto it and shimmied down, doing her best not to make any noise in the process. A moment later her shoes touched grass, then Matt was through the window and onto the pipe—anything but scrawny himself—and Tara had to wonder if the aluminum could handle the strain of his hard body.

It groaned in protest, a sound just loud enough to worry Tara. But despite the wound in his arm, Matt moved quickly and gracefully and, seconds later, was standing beside her.

Turning toward the rear of the house, they hustled into the backyard, vaulted a row of low bushes onto the neighbor's property, then headed for the street.

Chapter Sixteen

Once they were clear of Cop Country, they caught a cab to Tara's condo, and Matt waited with him as Tara ran upstairs to get some cash.

The ride over had been gloriously uneventful. The cabbie, a middle-aged guy wearing a Colorado Rockies cap, seemed more interested in his sports talk radio than he did in a couple of exhausted, disheveled passengers. He had barely glanced at them in his rearview mirror when they climbed in.

Even so, Matt had made sure to keep his head low. His face was plastered all over the news, and he could only hope that the cabbie hadn't been near a television set recently.

During the ride, Matt and Tara had barely said a word to each other. She had simply leaned into him and rested her head against his good shoulder, and he thought he could feel the tension in her body being released like a toxin, a slow but steady draining of the poisons.

His entire body felt tight, and he found himself wishing he could release his own tension. But he knew he wouldn't be able to relax until Jimmy Zane and his band of malcontents were put away.

His months behind bars, sharing a cell with Rusty Zane, lifting weights in the prison yard with Carl Maddox, would not be time spent in vain. He had worked too hard to get them to accept him. Had sacrificed a life of freedom, had done things inside that he wasn't particularly proud of, in order to get them to trust him.

And it had all been destroyed by Everhardt's betrayal.

The sight of him slumped in that chair had been like a knife to the gut.

But, in the end, Everhardt was no better than Carl or Rusty or Zane himself.

Without meaning to, Matt was suddenly thinking of the men who had shot and killed Becky and Jennifer.

Strangers. Even to this day.

A witness in the grocery store's parking lot had seen them enter just before the robbery and had described them to a police sketch artist.

The night manager, who had just come on duty, forgot to put a fresh tape into the store's antiquated video surveillance system, so the incident wasn't recorded, and the drawings were all the police had to go on.

Those drawings had been broadcast all over the local and state television news for a week straight, but nobody came forward to identify the two men.

Maybe that was a good thing. Because if Matt had been able to find out who they were, he would have personally hunted them down and put an end to their time on Earth without shedding a single tear for either one of them.

He was pretty sure the families of the other victims would have cheered him on.

But that was a long time ago. And the perpetrators had never been caught. Probably never would be. Not for that particular crime, at least.

Matt realized that the tension he felt right now was a tension he had carried with him for seven years. Unlike Tara, he couldn't let it go. It had seeped so far and so deep into his system that he had to wonder if it would stay with him forever.

He had learned to manage it. To keep it buried. But it was always there inside him, coiled and ready, and there was very little he could do about that but learn to live with it.

At moments like this, these moments of somber reflection, Matt would normally see Becky's and Jennifer's faces in his mind's eye.

But not this time.

For reasons he couldn't quite explain, he saw the face of the angel who had stared down at him in his dream. The face he had pressed his palm against as he lay in Imogene's shack.

Tara's face.

He wasn't sure why she had this effect on him. Couldn't put his feelings into words that were adequate enough to describe them. But when he thought of her face, when he thought of her body leaning into him, her head resting against his shoulder, the tension didn't quite disappear, but it *did* retreat for a moment.

Just long enough to give him hope.

Just long enough.

IT WAS A NIGHT FOR time warps.

The moment Tara stepped alone through her apartment doorway, she felt as if she'd been transported to a part of her life that no longer existed. One much less complicated. Less violent.

The post-modern furniture that dominated her living room with all of its hard angles and perfect lines, stood in sharp contrast to the ramshackle shack that she and Matt had been hiding in only hours ago.

Her keys were still in her car at The Brotherhood compound, so she got the night security man to let her in. Fortunately, he'd been working in her building for years and knew her by name.

Her condo was on the twenty-first floor, a large one-bedroom with bay windows and a panoramic view of the city. She wasn't a rich woman, but she'd managed to get a great deal on the place, and felt a certain pride of ownership every time she stepped foot inside.

Leaving the door open behind her, she crossed straight to the kitchen sideboard, pulled open one of the upper drawers and took out a small canister in which she had stored extra cash for emergencies. Removing several bills, she closed the drawer, then started back to the door, only to be stopped by the blinking of her message machine.

She punched a button and a mechanical voice announced she had one message waiting. When she pressed it again, she heard Susan's voice.

"Hey, sis, we tried calling you on your cell, but the reception up at the cabin is as terrible as always. Hope you're getting some rest. In the meantime, I've got a couple of monkeys here who want to say hello."

Tara smiled as the phone was handed off and two giggly, high-pitched voices came on the line, trying to speak in unison:

"Hi, Aunt Tara! Don't forget to come see us tomorrow! We love you!"

As they broke into squeals of laughter, Tara's heart

swelled. If she ever had kids of her own, she could only hope that they'd be half as cute as those two.

Susan came back on the line:

"Hope you get this message, kiddo. Nine o'clock sharp. We're assembling in the lobby."

As the line clicked off, Tara felt a stab of guilt.

Nine o'clock sharp.

At nine o'clock tomorrow she'd likely be halfway across town at the federal courthouse, watching Matt and the FBI take down The Brotherhood.

Assuming all went well, that is.

No guarantees at this point. If Matt didn't reach Abernathy soon, they might have to go straight to the police, and that could prove to be extremely problematic.

Matt had said it himself. Without confirmation that he was working undercover, the police weren't likely to take his warning of a homegrown terrorist attack too seriously.

And despite what Matt had said, Tara doubted they'd give *her* much credence, either. The police mistrusted anyone connected to television news. Especially in a time when that news was more about sensationalism than actual hard, fact-based reporting.

Besides, she was a hostage. One who was sympathetic to her captor, an escaped convict.

There were psychological terms for people like that.

They had considered going to the FBI itself, but

Matt knew from experience that, at well past midnight on a Friday night, they'd have to wade through more layers of bureaucracy than time would afford.

So everything hinged on contacting Abernathy.

Tara had suggested that they try his house, too, but Matt explained that Abernathy had moved recently and he had no idea where to find the guy.

It occurred to them that maybe Everhardt had done more than betray Matt to The Brotherhood. Maybe he had taken Abernathy out of the equation, as well.

And if that was the case, they were in deep trouble.

But as Tara grabbed her spare house key from a hook beside the door and headed toward the elevators, an idea struck her. One that might not convince the cops that Matt was who he claimed to be, but might embarrass them enough to at least check out his story.

At worst, it would alert the public that the possibility of danger existed.

And that, sometimes, was all you needed to prevent a disaster.

ONCE TARA HAD PAID the cabbie and joined Matt again, they decided to reenter her building through the underground parking lot. No point in letting the security man see Matt's face and decide to dial the police.

"What about surveillance cameras?" Matt asked.

Tara shook her head. "I've been complaining to the association for months that we need to upgrade the system to include the parking lot, but nobody seems to want to pay the additional fees."

Tara couldn't understand how people could put money before safety, but she saw it happen every day. Most of the tenants thought that locks and card keys were enough of a security precaution, and who was Tara to complain? At this particular point in time, their lack of concern was making life easier for her and Matt.

Moving down the ramp to the roll-away door, Tara inserted her key into a box mounted atop a pedestal in the center divider.

A moment later they were inside and headed to the elevator, the door rolling shut behind them.

WHEN THEY GOT INTO HER condo, Matt didn't waste time with any formalities. Spotting her landline, he went straight to it, picked it up and dialed a number.

Tara heard the line ringing again, but still no answer.

In a burst of anger, Matt clicked off and slammed the phone back into its cradle.

"Easy," Tara said, grabbing his forearm.

It took him a moment to get control of himself. She could see that he was wound tight and couldn't blame him for it. He had every right to be frustrated.

And scared. The thought that the lives of innocent bystanders might hinge on a single phone call would scare and frustrate anyone.

"One more hour," Matt said.

"Before what?"

"If I haven't made contact by then, we'll have to go to the police. I don't see any other way. We'll just have to take our chances and hope they believe us."

"Maybe we can give them a little nudge first."

Matt's brow furrowed. "Meaning what?"

"Don't forget what I do for a living," she said. "I'd have to wake up some people, but I could have a news crew here in less than an hour."

"What are you suggesting?"

"That we tell our story to the cameras. Your assignment, The Brotherhood, what happened to us and what they're planning. There's nothing more motivating to the police than the potential for bad publicity."

"It's past midnight," Matt said. "Who would be watching?"

"You'd be surprised. But it doesn't matter. As long as we're on record, the police are unlikely to ignore the warning. If they do, and something happens, then they look like fools. So the least they'll do is contact the FBI and hand us off to them."

"And the Bureau would be just as inclined to avoid

the bad publicity. God knows we've had our share of it over the years."

"Exactly," Tara said. "I don't really see a downside to this."

Matt nodded. "Let's not wait for Abernathy, then. Do it. Make the call."

Chapter Seventeen

Ron the Newscaster's cell phone rang and a woman picked up, groggy with sleep. "Hello?"

Tara was surprised. Candi the Weather Girl's voice was instantly recognizable, and for a moment she wondered if she'd dialed the wrong number.

But that didn't make sense. She'd used speed dial.

"Hey, Candi, this is Tara. Is Ron there?"

The grogginess instantly disappeared, replaced by a hint of embarrassment. "Oh, uh, yeah. Hi, Tara. I thought this was *my* phone. Hold on a sec."

Candi was a cute little redhead with a particular set of body attributes, top and bottom, that rendered most men helpless, turning them into blithering idiots who had only one thing on their minds. From the janitor all the way up to the station owner, just about every guy at KWEST was falling all over himself to get a date with her, and it looked as if Ron had snatched the prize.

And then some.

Tara figured she should probably be appalled with the way Candi had been so unapologetically objectified, but she couldn't help being amused by it.

Political correctness had never been her strong suit, anyway.

Ron came on the line a moment later, sounding alert. In the news business you never know when you'll have to be instantly awake, and Ron had trained himself well.

"I know what you're thinking," he said. "But don't say a word."

"I stopped caring about who you sleep with a long time ago, Ron. But I need you to get that butt of yours out of bed and over to my place as fast as humanly possible."

"Your place? I thought you were up at the cabin tonight."

"Long story," Tara said. "I'll tell you all about it when you get here. And bring a crew with you."

There was a pause. "Tara, what's going on?"

"Let's just say I'm about to make your career," she told him, then hung up.

When she turned, she discovered that Matt had moved to the sofa and was sitting down. He looked a bit pale, and a glance at his left arm told her why.

He was bleeding again. The makeshift bandage was soaked through.

"They should be here within the hour," she said.

"Good."

"Come into the bathroom. We need to get you properly patched up."

He shook his head. "I'll be fine."

"Are you always this stubborn?"

"You already know the answer to that. In fact, you know everything there is to know about me, remember? I'm a cop."

He was smiling, thought he was being funny, but Tara wasn't amused. She still felt ashamed for her comments earlier. It was true that she couldn't have known about Matt's past, but that didn't make her any less of an insensitive idiot.

"Look, I'm sorry I said what I did back at Imogene's place. Unfortunately, I have a fairly unique point of view on the matter. I'm a product of my environment."

"Aren't we all?" Matt said, then finally got to his feet. "So where's this bathroom? You lead, I follow."

"Be careful what you wish for."

She was using soap and water and a damp washcloth to clean Matt's wound when she realized he was staring at her.

"What?" she said, suddenly feeling defensive.

"Nothing."

He was perched on the sink with the mirror behind him, and she immediately looked at her reflection.

"The bruise?"

It had gotten worse, no doubt about it, a purplish blue-black monstrosity that seemed to have taken on a life of its own. Tara was reminded of a movie she'd once seen as a kid, about an amorphous blob that kept growing and growing, consuming everything in its path.

She wasn't big on makeup, but if she was going to be standing next to Matt in front of a camera crew, she might want to use a little cover-up.

But then she reconsidered. Always the producer, she decided it was better to leave the thing alone. The battered look would give them just the right touch of authenticity they needed.

"Not the bruise," Matt said. "Your eyes."

"What about them?"

He thought about it a moment, then shook his head. "Never mind. You'll just think I'm crazy."

She dropped the washcloth on the counter and frowned at him. "You start something like that, buster, you'd better be ready to finish. I'm already feeling self-conscious enough as it is. I don't need you adding fuel to the fire."

"All right," he said. "Just remember I warned you."

"How could I possibly forget?"

He shifted uncomfortably on the countertop. "I don't normally say stuff like this. I'm one of those kind of guys where what you see is what you get. I don't write poetry, I don't sing love songs, I tell the truth as I see it and sometimes I'm blunt to a fault."

"You also take forever to get to the point."

"It's just that, ever since I met you, whenever I look into your eyes, when I take a moment like this to *really* see what's behind them, I…" He paused, as if wanting to get the words just right. "I guess you could say I see myself. All the fears, all the vulnerabilities, but all the strengths, too. It's like you're part of me. In a way I don't quite understand. There's a connection between us that seems to go back beyond our years. If I believed in such things, I'd say we knew each other in a previous life."

Tara's brow furrowed. Everything he'd said had tugged at her heart, until that last part. She suddenly wasn't sure what he was trying to tell her.

"Previous life?" she said. "What exactly does that mean? You think I'm Becky?"

Matt closed his eyes, shook his head. "No. God, no. Becky and I… I don't know how to say this without sounding like a complete jerk, but what Becky and I had was never exactly earth-shattering. I loved her, and I miss her, and I wish to God she were still alive, but…we were friends more than anything else. And the glue that held us together was Jennifer. Without her, I don't know how long we would have lasted."

Tara looked at him, and could see that every word he'd spoken was heartfelt. Genuine.

He cupped her chin, held her gaze. His own green-gray eyes were burning with an intensity that made it impossible to look away.

Not that she wanted to. She could stay here forever and would relish every single moment of it.

"But when I look at *you*," he said quietly, "I see something I've never seen before. Something real." Another pause. "As crazy as it sounds...I see my soul."

Then he kissed her.

Softly, at first, then again with more urgency as he slid off the counter and pulled her into his arms, his hands sliding under the V-neck, brushing against her rib cage, then up along her back.

His tongue found hers and the kiss deepened, a stutter of electricity rolling through her body—a current so strong that, for a moment, she wondered if she could handle it. Something loosened inside of her, something wet and warm and so exquisitely wonderful that she thought she must be dreaming.

She had never felt such a sensation before. Not like this. Not with Ron, not with Eric the Architect. This man was awakening something inside her that she had never known existed.

It was as if she had been administered some new type of drug, a powerful intoxicant that somehow rendered all rational thought meaningless. Irrelevant. A drug that sluiced through the bloodstream like fire and ice, making her body react in ways she couldn't quite describe.

Then, as if each could read the other's mind, they both stepped away from the kiss and moved into the bedroom.

Standing at the foot of Tara's bed, they began by removing each other's clothes, Matt grabbing the hem of the V-neck and pulling it over her head in one fluid motion.

She returned the favor, exposing his hard chest and abdomen, and that long scar that she had felt so compelled to touch in Imogene's shack.

She didn't hold back this time and ran her fingers along it, feeling its heat, its history, wanting to put her lips there, to taste the tortured flesh, to let him feel the flicker of her tongue against it.

But before she could act on that impulse, he had her left breast in his hand, gently cupping it, leaning forward to draw the hard nipple between his lips.

Then he sank into a crouch, pressing his lips against her stomach, bringing his hands up to unfasten her jeans, then shoving them down past her thighs, her knees, her ankles.

She stepped out of them and the panties came next.

He paused for a moment to run his tongue along her pelvic bone, to linger there, the electricity deepening and widening and threatening to devour her so completely that she was almost afraid she'd never recover.

Almost.

He stood up again, then sat her on the edge of the bed and removed his own jeans and boxers, and she could see that he was ready for her, as ready as she *felt*. She grabbed hold of him, feeling his heat, his hardness, the throbbing urgency beneath the flesh.

Leaning forward, she drew him into her mouth, using her teeth and tongue to tease him, and he groaned, a guttural, animal-like sound that only heightened her passion.

When neither of them could wait any longer, she fell back on the mattress and he grabbed her knees, parting her thighs, lifting her slightly off the bed as he entered her, pushing deep, a feeling so right and so wonderful that any doubts she'd felt about this man vanished in an instant.

And as amazing as it felt to have him inside her, to feel him on top of her, flesh against flesh, his lips pressed against her neck, her shoulders, her breasts, it was the words she remembered, the words he had spoken with such unabashed sincerity that she couldn't deny them. Didn't *want* to deny them.

In any other context they might be the corniest

words ever uttered, but they had been meant for her, only her, coming from a man who brought to the surface feelings and emotions Tara had never before felt.

When I look at you...

I see my soul.

And it was true.

She saw *her* soul, too. Felt as if they were connected by some unseen, unspoken force. A shared emotional history, an understanding of what it means to be alone.

And maybe he *was* her soul mate.

Her Henry.

Matt's breathing began to quicken now and she sensed that, like her, he was close. Very close. A wave of pleasure rolled through her, threatening to capsize her and carry her away.

And in that moment, Tara knew that no matter what happened after this, if this night were never to be repeated, was merely the merging of two wounded souls in search of temporary refuge from a lonely and violent world...she would never forget it.

Would never regret it.

Would always remember it as the most exhilarating night of her life.

MATT LAY STILL NOW, breathing quietly beside her. Tara snaked her arm around him, kissed his cheek, then let her hand drop down, brushing her nails against him, teasing him.

Unfortunately, there was no time for a repeat performance. Not if they wanted to look presentable for Ron and his crew.

"Shower," she said. "We both need one."

"Is that a command or an invitation?"

She laughed against his neck. Kissed him there. "Both. We'll save time if we go in together."

So that's what they did, sharing Tara's bar of rose petal soap, lathering up each other. Then Matt grabbed the shave cream and squirted her, a pile of foam gathering on her neck and breasts.

They laughed and laughed hard, as Tara wiped the foam from her chest and smeared it on his face, smashing his nose with her palm.

And then suddenly, still in perfect sync, they both stopped laughing and stared at each other.

Said nothing for a long moment.

Let the water cascade over their bodies.

Reaching up, Matt gingerly touched her bruise, then put his lips there, as if to kiss away the pain. Then he kissed the tip of her nose, her lips, and she turned away and pressed her backside into him, feeling him grow against her, wanting him again, wanting him inside her.

A moment later, she got her wish.

And the wave came crashing into her, harder and faster than ever before.

AS MUCH AS TARA HATED the idea of Matt wearing his filthy clothes again, they didn't have a choice. She had nothing to replace them with.

Besides, considering that he'd be pleading his case on camera any minute now, it was probably best to keep him in character, as calculating as that might sound.

Tara knew from long experience that the viewing public made far too many snap judgments based on first impressions, and if a freshly laundered escaped convict were to show up on camera, they'd likely smell a rat. It was bad enough that she and Matt had taken a shower, but she couldn't have gone another minute without one.

Maybe she was overanalyzing all of this. Who really cared what the public thought? Their only goal here was to spur the police into taking action against The Brotherhood.

When Matt was dressed, he squeezed her hand and said, "I'll try Abernathy one more time."

As he went into the living room, Tara ran a comb through her freshly washed hair, then checked the clock on her nightstand, wondering why her doorbell hadn't yet rung.

Ron and his crew should have been here by now.

And as she crossed to her bedroom doorway, she heard a sound, jerked her head up.

Her front door burst open and a platoon of Sheriff's deputies crashed into the room wearing helmets and flak jackets, their automatic weapons pointed straight at Tara and Matt.

"Down!" one of them shouted. "Noses to the floor! Get down! Now!"

Before Tara could fully comprehend what was happening, she was facedown on the carpet, the barrel of an automatic rifle touching the back of her head as her arms were jerked behind her and nylon cuffs were wrapped around her wrists.

"Don't even flinch, lady. You're under arrest for harboring a fugitive."

Chapter Eighteen

Jimmy Zane was watching television when someone knocked on his office door.

The satellite signal, which had been hacked and cloned by one of his men in the computer pool, was coming in clean and clear tonight. This pleased Zane, because it gave him a chance to watch his plan in action. A plan he had been working on for two long years.

A special bulletin played out on-screen, a report on the capture of prison escapee and wanted fugitive, Nick Stanton. Stanton was found at the apartment of one Tara Richmond, a KWEST Television news producer—which was ironic, since the reporter covering the arrest was KWEST's most trusted news anchor, Ron Michaels.

The video footage, with a fancy graphic that read RECORDED EARLIER, showed Stanton and Richmond being perp-walked in handcuffs to a pair of Sheriff's patrol cars. The news anchor watched in stunned disbelief, a look of unscripted horror on his makeup-caked face.

Despite that horror, however, he managed to keep babbling. "Sheriff's deputies say they were tipped by an anonymous caller as to the whereabouts of convicted murderer, Nick Stanton. The question of Ms. Richmond's involvement remains unclear, but sources close to the investigation say that she could be charged with aiding and abetting a fugitive from justice."

Zane detested men like Michaels. He detested all reporters, who only existed to feed on the misery of others in order to sell bottles of beer or prescription drugs or shiny new hybrid cars and SUVs.

They were vultures, plain and simple. Birds of prey who were more interested in sensationalism than the truth. Who hovered over the carcasses of the disadvantaged and the misunderstood, picking at their bones in search of a story, *any* story, that would keep their viewers glued to the screen.

They'd have that story tomorrow.

And there would plenty of carcasses to choose from.

Someone knocked again, but Zane ignored it, watching the arrest play out on the screen, amused by something he had just noticed.

Stanton—aka Special Agent Matt Hathaway— was wearing a Marine-green T-shirt with the words NEVER SURRENDER written across the chest.

There was a third knock and Zane sighed. He hated being interrupted at times like this. Much of his work was done in the wee hours, when he could be alone with this thoughts, the pressures of running a command like The Brotherhood momentarily lifted.

But not tonight, apparently.

Frowning now, he grabbed the remote, flicked off the television and called out, "Yes? What is it?"

The door opened and Cameron, one of his best lieutenants, stuck his head inside the room. "We have Maddox."

"Where?"

"Right outside."

Zane tossed the remote to the desktop and nodded. "Bring him in."

A moment later, Cameron returned with two security men who held Carl Maddox by the arms as they marched him into the room.

Zane gestured and they sat Maddox down in a chair in front of the desk.

Maddox was scowling. As defiant as always.

"Leave us," Zane said to his men.

"Do you want him cuffed?"

Zane shook his head. "That won't be necessary."

With a quick salute, Cameron and the security men left the room. Zane returned the salute, then studied Maddox silently, half expecting the idiot to blurt out something in his own defense, to try to weasel out of what was a clear violation of The Brotherhood's code.

But Maddox said nothing. Simply stared at Zane from across the desk, his eyes hard and his jaw set.

Zane leaned forward in his chair.

"What possessed you," he asked, "to disobey a direct order?"

Maddox's gaze didn't waver. "Which order was that?"

"Don't be coy with me, soldier. I told you not to go after the traitor and the girl, but you chose to ignore my command. A breach that could have been detrimental to our entire plan."

"Detrimental?" Maddox said. "What are you talking about? The guy's a *federal agent*. He could expose *everything*."

"That's exactly what I want him to do."

Maddox's eyes widened and he leaned forward in his chair. "You *what?*"

"We're playing chess here, Carl. Not tiddledywinks. And even when you have a sound strategy and surprise on your side, sometimes a subtle bit of misdirection is necessary to throw off your opponent."

"What the heck are you talking about?"

"The feds have a strong presence in Whitestone," Zane said. "Not to mention the local Sheriff's department and SWAT team. When I found out the FBI was attempting to infiltrate our organization, I could have pulled the plug on the entire operation right then and there, but that would have been admitting defeat before we'd even gone to war. So then I thought, why not counter their move in a way that would get them to focus their attention in another direction entirely? One that would broadcast their incompetence to the world. That's why I let you and Rusty bring the traitor here in the first place."

Maddox shook his head in confusion and disgust. "You've lost me completely."

"I know that, Carl. That's why I give the orders and you obey them. And I don't like being second-guessed."

"Well cry me a freakin' river. Nobody tells me what to do."

Zane smiled, but it wasn't meant to be friendly. There was no mirth in it whatsoever.

He was losing his patience with Maddox, but despite the man's flaws, Maddox was also a patriot. And as far as Zane was concerned, every patriot deserved a second chance.

Assuming he was willing to accept the conditions.

"Know this," he told Carl. "And I'll say it in terms even someone of your limited intellectual capacity can comprehend." He paused. "If you *ever* disobey an order again, if you *ever* so much as say a contrary word to me, I will have you shot. Do you understand?"

Maddox opened his mouth to protest, but Zane left no room for disagreement.

"Do. You. Understand?"

Maddox swallowed, looking considerably paler and less defiant than he had when he was first brought into the office. He slowly nodded. "Yes, sir."

"I can't hear you, soldier."

"Yes, sir!" Carl shouted. "I understand."

"Excellent," Zane said. "Since Rusty's no good to me with his leg the way it is, I'll need you on point tomorrow, without the attitude. You have any objections to that?"

He expected a protest, but it didn't come.

Smiling now, he got to his feet. He'd had enough of this moron.

But before he could dismiss Maddox, his office door flew open and a familiar figure stood in the doorway, a scowl on her weathered face.

"Mother," Zane said in surprise. "I didn't expect you back so soon."

The old woman's gaze shot directly past Zane and zeroed in on Maddox. "You and your boys almost killed me out there."

Maddox's eyebrows went up. "That was *you?*"

"Yes, you little pinhead. And I don't like being shot at."

Then Imogene Zane walked into the room and slapped Carl square across the face.

Chapter Nineteen

They put them in separate interrogation rooms.

Except for one brief moment back at Imogene's shack, it was the first time since this crazy night began that Matt hadn't had Tara at his side, and he felt naked without her.

More than that, actually. He felt as if a vital part of him were missing.

Funny how your entire life could change in a few short hours. How something you never thought would happen to you could happen so abruptly and so completely that you mistrusted it at first, only to later realize how foolish you'd been for not recognizing it immediately.

He was in love with her.

Wanted to be with her for the rest of his life.

It was that simple.

And ever since she had been taken away from him, ever since they had been handcuffed and escorted to separate patrol cars, he had felt lost and incomplete.

Sooner or later, he would see Tara again.

But he felt empty nevertheless.

They had left him alone in this room for over an hour now, not a word spoken to him since the arrest—a course of action that was meant to unnerve and disarm him. And when you're alone for so long with only your thoughts for company, you tend to drift toward self-analysis and personal reflection.

As they were putting him in the patrol car, he had tried to tell them who he really was, to contact the FBI, to reach Abernathy. But just as he had feared, they hadn't listened. He was a wanted fugitive, a danger to society, and anything he might say would be regarded with suspicion and routinely ignored.

Matt knew the playbook.

Knew all the moves.

He'd made them himself more times than he could remember.

They would let him stew in here for a while, then they'd start to sweat him, questioning him over and over until he finally broke down and gave them exactly what they wanted: the whereabouts of Rusty Zane and Carl Maddox.

And while he knew he could give them the approximate coordinates of The Brotherhood's compound, he also knew that sending them into the mountains would be a time-consuming distraction, and there were matters here in the city that needed their immediate attention.

So, with or without Abernathy, he had to convince these men that he was not who they thought he was.

And experience told him that this wouldn't be easy.

TARA HAD FALLEN ASLEEP again, but there were no dreams this time. Just a blissful, blank, unfettered loss of consciousness, as she sat chained to a chair in a room not much bigger than a walk-in closet.

She wasn't sure how they'd been caught. Her first instinct was that Ron had turned them in, but she knew that couldn't be true. She hadn't told him about Matt when she called him. She also liked to believe that he'd never do that to her.

But once she dismissed that thought, a picture of Imogene entered her mind. As they were being escorted to the patrol cars, she was almost sure she had seen an old Rambler out of the corner of her eye. Parked down the street.

Was it the old woman's car?

Had she followed them, then called the police?

And if she had, then why? Why would she help them, only to turn around and betray them later?

It made no sense.

After bringing Tara to the station, the police had kept her in this room for a long time. She had tried calling out to them, telling them that they were making a mistake, a mistake that could cost the lives of innocent people.

But if they were listening, they didn't care. All of her protests, even those fired at the back of a deputy's head in the patrol car, had been ignored.

It was, she thought, typical cop behavior. The kind of thing she'd experienced time and again as she was growing up. An inbred arrogance that said, *I'm right, you're wrong, end of discussion.*

Not this time, however.

Not if she could help it.

"Hey!" she shouted. "Hey, you out there!" She looked up at the video camera mounted in a high corner. "Are you going to let me sit here all night, or grow a pair and start asking me some—"

The door flew open behind her and a man in rolled-up shirtsleeves strolled into the room, dropping a brown manila folder onto the tabletop.

"Good morning, Ms. Richmond. I'm Detective Roderick Wilkins. I'll be handling your debriefing."

"It's about time."

"My apologies for making you wait. Things tend to move a little less briskly around here at this time of morning."

"Then you'd better start picking it up," Tara said. "Because what I'm about to tell you will require you to immediately mobilize every resource you have."

"Oh, we're mobilized, believe me. Ninety percent for our force is out there in the streets, looking for Rusty Zane and Carl Maddox."

"Those two are the least of your worries. And if you think grabbing Matt and me is some kind of feather in your cap, you can—"

"Who?"

"Matt. Matt Hathaway. *Special Agent* Matt Hathaway, the man you arrested in my apartment. He's working undercover for the FBI."

Wilkins smiled slightly, trying and failing to hide his amusement. It was a look that made Tara want to scratch his eyes out.

"So is that what Stanton told you? Is that the story he used to get you to go along with him?"

"It's not a story, it's the truth."

"And I assume he showed you proof of this?"

Tara hesitated. Matt *hadn't* shown her any proof, but she trusted him. Knew he wouldn't lie to her. Besides, she'd heard the words come out of Zane's own mouth:

My man tells me he's Famous But Incompetent.

Why would Zane have said this about Matt if it weren't true? And why would they have been running around in the woods all night getting shot at?

"Have you ever heard of the term Stockholm Syndrome?" Wilkins asked.

"Of course I have."

"Then you know it's not uncommon for victims of abduction to grow sympathetic toward their captors."

Tara shook her head. "That isn't what's happened here."

"So are you denying that the two of you were intimate?"

Tara hesitated again. Just long enough to make it clear what her answer was.

"You *were* intimate with him, weren't you?"

She felt herself blush once again, but pushed past it.

"Matt Hathaway is not who you think he is," she said. "He's been working deep undercover for almost a year now. His handlers were two agents named Everhardt and Abernathy, but Everhardt is dead now and—"

The detective frowned at her and cut her off. "We had a call about a victim named Everhardt earlier tonight. A suicide. How could you possibly know about that?"

"That's exactly what I'm trying to tell you. Everhardt was one of Matt's handlers. And if you contact the FBI and get them to round up Agent Abernathy, you'll know this is all a terrible mistake. The Brotherhood is planning to blow up the federal courthouse tomorrow and if you don't turn the focus of this investigation in that direction, a lot of people will wind up dead."

Another look of amusement. "The Brotherhood, huh?"

"That's what they call themselves."

"Then why haven't I heard of them before?"

"I don't know," Tara said. "Maybe because they like to fly under the radar. Does it really matter? All that counts is that the FBI knows about them and they sent Matt to prison to try to infiltrate the—"

"All right, Ms. Richmond. Enough fairy tales."

"It's not a fairy tale. People are in danger."

"Look," Wilkins said, "it's obvious to me that you've bought into this ridiculous conspiracy theory because of your feelings for Stanton, sexual or otherwise. And when I think about it, you work at a news station, you could easily have learned about Everhardt's suicide from them. It's fairly big news." Tara started to protest, but he held a hand up. "Let me finish."

She closed her mouth. It didn't really matter what she told him, this jerk would never believe her anyway.

I'm right, you're wrong, end of story.

Wilkins opened the manila folder in front of him and slid it across the table to Tara. "This is the man you've invested yourself in." He gestured. "Take a look."

It was a typical police file, the kind Tara had seen a hundred different times. But this one featured a mug shot of Matt, his eyes hard and cold as he stared into the camera.

It was a look that made her shiver.

If she didn't know Matt was playing a part, she might be frightened by it.

"The guy's an arms dealer and a stone-cold killer," Wilkins said. "Shot two police officers and a federal agent when his warehouse was raided. So don't give me any more nonsense about undercover missions and militant organizations. This guy's a bad guy no matter how you slice it."

Tara stared at the report, then closed the folder and looked up at Wilkins.

"All right," she said. "No more BS—I can tell you where to find the other two. Zane and Maddox."

Wilkins smiled. "I knew you had some sense in you. You being a cop's daughter and all."

"I'm glad you brought that up," Tara said, "because there's a condition to my cooperation."

"Which is?"

"I don't want to deal with you anymore. From here on out, the only one I'll talk to is my father's widow. Detective Lila Sinclair."

Chapter Twenty

Tara had no idea what time it was when Lila walked into the room.

Before she and the detective arrived at the station house, all Tara could think about was how quickly the minutes were passing, each one more crucial than the last.

She didn't know what was going on with Matt, either. She assumed that he was in one of the other interrogation rooms, telling them the same story she'd told Wilkins. But she had a feeling they'd be listening to him even less than they'd listened to her.

When it came down to it, she really couldn't blame them. On paper it all seemed so obvious. Nick Stanton was a hardened criminal who had escaped from prison, and until they had evidence to the contrary, they'd go with what they knew.

Police organizations were territorial by nature, and they'd see no point in bringing in the FBI unless they could be convinced that it was absolutely necessary.

And it would undoubtedly take a lot to convince them of that.

Unless Tara managed to use her trump card.

Lila was an attractive woman with a trim figure, wearing jeans, a simple dress shirt and a corduroy jacket.

Detective-wear 101.

She closed the door behind her, her voice soft, well modulated. "Hello, Tara."

Tara stiffened slightly. As she watched Lila pull out a chair and sit down, she found herself caught up in yet another time warp, remembering that Thanksgiving dinner so long ago, and how Lila had barely put anything on her plate.

Who comes to Thanksgiving dinner, Tara had wondered, and doesn't eat?

Now that she thought about it, however, the fact that you're sleeping with the guy whose wife just cooked the meal might make you lose your appetite.

There was an awkward silence as the two women assessed each other. It was clear that Lila had no idea why she was here, why Tara would choose *her*, of all people, to confess her sins to.

But Tara had no intension of confessing anything.

She wanted a favor.

She nodded to the camera mounted in the high

corner. "Can you have them turn that thing off? I want to talk to you privately for a moment."

Lila looked surprised, but didn't hesitate. She gestured with a finger and the camera's blinking red light went dark.

Then Tara said, "I'm curious."

"About what?"

"What my father told you about me. What kind of person he thought I was."

"I don't see how that's relevant right now."

"Oh, it's relevant," Tara told her. "Did he say I was a liar? Did he ever tell you that I make up stories? That I can't be trusted?"

Lila shook her head. "None of those things. Just the opposite, in fact."

"Good."

"And on a personal note," Lila said, "when it comes to me, you've never hesitated to express how you feel."

That was certainly true. Tara was all too happy to share her opinion about Lila, and some of the words she'd used in the past were not kind or ladylike.

"I guess I was pretty rude to you at the funeral, wasn't I?"

"You could say that, yeah."

Tara just looked at her. "If you expect me to say I'm sorry, I won't."

"I'm not asking you to," Lila said. "I pretty much

deserved it. It was stupid of me to get involved with Ed the way I did. We should have waited until he'd worked out all of his personal problems."

"Is that some kind of apology?"

Lila shrugged. "If you want to call it that, sure."

Tara was surprised by this. She had always looked at this woman as the dragon lady, but maybe Lila didn't deserve that. Maybe she was just another lonely person wanting someone to love her. Was it her fault that Tara's father had turned out to be that someone?

Maybe he had been *her* Henry.

One thing Tara had learned as a news producer was that every story had multiple sides, and looking at the world from different perspectives was usually an eye-opening experience. Maybe if she were to walk in Lila's shoes for a while, she wouldn't be so quick to judge the woman.

"If you really want to apologize," she said, "you can do me a favor."

Lila's guard went up. Just a subtle shift in her eyes, but Tara saw it. A move from personal to professional. "What kind of favor?"

"I want you to think about how I express my feelings. How I don't lie. How I can be trusted. But most of all, I want you to think of me as your late husband's daughter."

"And?"

"I need you to make a phone call. A simple phone call, that's all I ask."

"And who exactly am I calling?"

Tara looked at her, hoping her request wouldn't immediately be shot down.

"The FBI," she said.

THEY FOUND SPECIAL AGENT Abernathy in bed.

He had spent Friday on an all-day hike and had come home exhausted, fighting what he thought might be the flu, with just enough energy to take a quick shower and slide between the sheets.

He didn't know about Everhardt. Hadn't heard about the prison break.

The ringer on his cell phone, it turned out, had been inadvertently switched off. But even if it hadn't been, he doubted he would have heard it ringing.

After taking Lila Sinclair's phone call, the FBI had done some checking and found no record of an Agent Matt Hathaway, or any alleged undercover operation. But the mention of Frank Everhardt's suicide message—with startling accuracy, thanks to Tara—had made them perk up and take notice. Everhardt was a commander of an antiterrorist task force whose activities had been highly secretive in nature.

And after a look at his computer files, they not only discovered a memo mentioning Hathaway, Abernathy and The Brotherhood, but found that Everhardt had somehow secured unauthorized access to the FBI personnel database and case files.

Special Agent Abernathy had no idea that any of this was going on until his bedroom door burst open and two fellow agents rousted him out of bed.

By the time he got to the Whitestone Sheriff's station and brought everyone up to speed, it was very close to eight o'clock.

An hour before detonation.

WHEN MATT EMERGED from the interrogation room, bleary-eyed and tired after hours of endless questioning, he saw Abernathy standing there and didn't think he'd ever been happier to see someone in his entire life, with the possible exception of Tara, who stood just beyond the agent, next to an attractive older woman in a corduroy jacket.

After shaking Abernathy's hand, Matt went straight to her and pulled her into a hug, feeling as if he'd never let her go.

"This is all because of you, isn't it?"

"Doesn't hurt to have enemies in high places," she said.

Chapter Twenty-One

Watching law enforcement mobilize was a sight to
see. Men and women in flak jackets and helmets,
automatic weapons slung over their shoulders, working with military precision as they checked their gear
and pile into dark, unmarked SUVs.

Before his assignment undercover, Matt had been
part of many such mobilizations, from DEA drug
raids, to surrounding a bank in a hostage situation.

As he watched what looked like the entire Sheriff's
department move into action, planning a simultane-
ous attack on The Brotherhood's compound and the
federal courthouse, Matt felt the adrenaline starting to pump through his veins. The moment he had
worked toward for nearly a year was finally coming
to fruition.

But not, it turned out, for him.

"You're officially off duty," Abernathy told him as
they stood amid the scramble of bodies and vehicles
in the Sheriff's Department parking lot.

"What are you talking about?" Matt said. "If it weren't for Tara and me, none of this would be happening right now."

"I know that. But I also know that you're hurt, you're exhausted, and the condition you're in, you'd probably be more of a hindrance than a help."

"You've got to be joking."

"I wish I were," Abernathy said. "But I can't risk you being out in the field. So I'm ordering you to go to the hospital, get some stitches in that arm, then go home and get some rest. There'll be plenty of mop-up to take care of tomorrow."

"Mop-up? That's all I'm good for?"

"This is not a reflection on the work you've done, Matt. You can expect more than your share of commendations for this."

Matt scowled at him. "I couldn't care less about commendations. I just want to see Zane's face when we bring him down."

A black SUV pulled up beside them, and the rear passenger door opened, beckoning to the agent.

"You'll see enough of Zane's face when you testify against him," Abernathy said. "My order stands."

Then he was inside the SUV and gone, leaving Matt behind.

Cursing under his breath, Matt crossed the lot to the nearest Sheriff's deputy, who had stowed his weapon and was about to climb into his cruiser.

"You're headed to the courthouse, right?"

"That's right," the deputy told him.

"You think I could hitch a ride with you?"

The deputy was about to respond when a large KWEST news van pulled up next to Matt and the side door slid open.

It was Tara, surrounded by shelves full of electronic gear, the cross-chatter of a police radio rising behind her. "What happened? Where's Abernathy?"

"He cut me loose. Says I'm in no condition for duty."

She frowned, then gestured. "Get in."

Matt didn't have to be told twice. He climbed in and she closed the door after him, signaling for the driver to get them out of there.

A bombshell redhead rode shotgun, while a newscaster that Matt recognized from TV—Ron Something-or-other—crouched next to her. Tara quickly introduced them. "This is your lucky day," she said. "You get to see me doing what I do best."

Matt smiled. "And here I thought you hit your pinnacle in the shower."

Tara's face lit up with embarrassment and she shook her head. "You've just proven that you're definitely all male."

"I didn't prove it before?"

Tara patted his chest. "Let's stick to the matter

at hand, tough guy. We'll talk about the other stuff later."

Then she pecked him on the nose and told the driver to hurry it up.

THE FEDERAL COURTHOUSE was a good twenty minutes from the Sheriff's station, and the clock on the van's dash told Tara that they didn't have much more time than that.

Assuming, of course, Zane hadn't abandoned his plan.

But Tara didn't think so. Even though Zane knew that she and Matt were on the loose, the guy had seemed just arrogant enough to go forward with the detonation anyway. His way of showing the federal government a giant middle finger.

But when Tara thought it through, there was something about that idea that didn't sit quite right.

Something off.

A notion that had been gnawing at her ever since they'd been perp-walked to the Sheriff's patrol cars.

"Did you happen to ask any of the deputies how they found us?"

"A couple of times, yeah."

"And?"

"They mostly ignored me," Matt said, "but one of them did mention an anonymous phone call. I never got any details."

Tara nodded. "I think it may have been Imo-gene."

"Imogene? Why?"

"I thought I saw her car when we were arrested."

"I'm sure you're mistaken."

"No," Tara said. "I'm pretty sure I'm right. And you were asleep when she said this, but when she was bringing us back into the city, she had some pretty harsh words about the police that reminded me of Carl and the Zanes."

Matt squinted at her. "Where are you headed with this?"

"The only direction that makes any sense."

"Which is?"

The scenario tumbled through Tara's mind, thoughts piling on top of one another so quickly that she could barely find a way to organize them.

She tried anyway.

"I keep looking for a reason why Imogene would go to all the trouble to help us, only to wind up turn-ing us in."

"Assuming she did," Matt said. "And you have no proof of that."

"Who else is there? The security man at my build-ing never saw you, and the only person who even knew you were in the city was Imogene. She probably called the police at Everhardt's house, but when that didn't work, she figured out where we'd go next and tried again."

"Even if you're right, it still doesn't tell me why."

"Think about it," Tara said. "What if we were set up? What if our escape, the romp in the woods, Imogene taking us through the mine—what if all of that was planned somehow?"

"That's crazy. It would be impossible to coordinate something like that."

"Would it? Maybe not to the letter, there'd be a whole lot of variables to deal with, but if Zane *wanted* us to get to the city, it wouldn't be all that tough to engineer. For all we know, he put some kind of tracking device on us. Which would explain how Imogene found us in that shack, and at my condo."

Matt said nothing. Seemed to be running the idea through his head, weighing its value. Then he began patting his jeans, his face changing expression as he found something and reached into his right back pocket.

"I don't believe it," he said, looking stunned, then held up a tiny black nodule, about half the size of a pencil eraser. He studied it closely. "This looks military grade."

"Still think I'm crazy?"

"No, but I'm still wondering *why*. Why would Zane go to all this trouble?"

"It's Saturday, right?"

"That's the rumor, yeah."

"So tell me, who goes to the federal courthouse on Saturdays?"

"No one. It's closed."

"So why bomb a building that's unoccupied?"

Matt shook his head, shrugged. "To minimize the casualties."

Tara raised an eyebrow. "Does Jimmy Zane strike you as the kind of guy who cares about casualties? 'Collateral damage,' remember? 'We hold the power.' The more people you kill, the more power you hold." She paused. "And one other thing."

"What?"

"Zane said the bombs were structural. That they'd been planted inside the building. Do you know how hard it would be to set that up in a working federal courthouse?"

"Practically impossible," Matt said.

"Exactly."

Tara could see that he was with her now. His mind seemed to be racing.

"So the courthouse isn't Zane's target," he said. "He knew he was being infiltrated, so he decided to use us to his advantage. We divert the forces while he's across town, taking down another building and making us all look like fools."

"A building with tons of collateral damage," Tara said. And the moment the words passed her lips, she realized what Zane's real target was, her chest seizing up with panic.

The Performing Arts Center.

She swiveled around to the workbench behind her and flipped on a television monitor. KWEST was televising the dedication ceremony, which would be starting very soon, and on-screen was a shot of the center's lobby, crowded with people, including a handful of celebrities and some local and national politicians.

Susan and Kyle were in there somewhere, too. Along with Kelly and Kimberly.

Oh my God.

Tara's gut told her she was right, but she needed proof. "Call the station," she told them. "Tell them to pipe down the archival footage of the arts center being built."

Ron got on the phone and a moment later the download was ready and Tara was fast-forwarding through it, watching the screen intently.

When she saw what she was looking for, she paused the footage and pointed to the screen.

"Any guesses what Imogene said her son does for a living?"

On the screen was a shot of the Performing Arts

Center, only half built. And parked out front was a large container truck marked RGB CONSTRUCTION.

The very same truck they'd seen at The Brotherhood compound.

Chapter Twenty-Two

They couldn't get through to the arts center on their cell phones.

Matt had already called Abernathy to tell him about their suspicions, and Abernathy had decided to reroute half their forces across town.

Hopefully, it wouldn't be too late.

But when Tara tried to call Susan and Kyle, she got no signal.

Same problem with the arts center security office.

"Zane must be jamming the radio frequency," Matt said. "And judging by the quality of that tracker, he's using high-end equipment to do it."

Tara could barely control her panic. "My nieces are in that building. We have to warn them. Get them out of there." She turned to the driver. "Hurry, Joe, hurry!"

The driver jammed his foot against the accelerator and the van shot forward, weaving in and out of traffic.

"Speaking of the tracker," Matt said, "if Zane sees we're headed away from the courthouse, he may trigger the detonator early."

Moving to the front of the van, Matt threw the device out the window.

"That should keep him guessing for a while."

Ron the Newscaster checked the road ahead, then shouted back to them. "Only about half a mile to go."

IT SEEMED MORE LIKE twenty miles, and by the time they reached the building, Tara's heart felt as if it might literally burst out of her chest.

Before the van even came to a stop, Matt had the side door open and he and Tara were jumping out, racing across a wide expanse of cement to the arts center entrance.

Pedestrians were milling around the courtyard, and they had to weave in and out, dodging bodies.

Matt gestured to Tara, indicating a nearby security car. "I'll let them know what's happening," he said. "You go inside and get everyone out of the building."

"What do I tell them?"

"The truth."

"But I'll start a panic. They'll go crazy."

"Better than the alternative," Matt said, and then he was cutting sideways, headed for the security car.

Tara burst through the lobby doorways, only to find that the place was huge and packed to the gills, patrons drinking champagne and orange juice, munching on bite-sized breakfast snacks. A podium was set up on the stage at the back of the room.

She checked a clock on the wall above it.

Eight-fifty-three a.m.

"Everyone, listen up!" she shouted.

But the ceiling was high and the crowd noise drowned out her voice.

"Everyone, listen!" she tried again, and a few nearby patrons stared at her as if she'd just lost her mind.

She desperately scanned the crowd for Susan and the twins. A group of preschool children stood near the stage, but no Kelly or Kimberly.

"This is an emergency!" she shouted. "Everyone needs to clear out of the building! Now!"

Eight-fifty-four a.m.

The few people who had heard her studied her with great concern, then turned and chattered to one another as if trying to decide what to do.

Should they believe her?

Some of them started moving toward the doorways, but the clock was ticking and this wasn't going nearly fast enough.

There was a microphone on the podium. Tara knew she had to get to it.

She pushed her way through the crowd, working toward the back of the room. She was halfway there when she bumped into a woman in a yellow sundress, and realized with relief that it was Susan.

Oh my God, Susan.

Her sister turned, surprise in her eyes.

"Tara!" she beamed. "You made it! I've been trying to call you all..." She stopped herself. "What happened to your face?"

"Where are the twins?"

"Why? What's wrong?"

"Where *are* they?"

Susan frowned. "Kelly spilled orange juice on her dress. Kyle took them to the restroom. What's going on? You're scaring me."

Tara grabbed her by the shoulders. "You *should* be scared. Listen to me carefully. I don't have time to explain, but you need to help me get everyone out of here. Right now."

"What are you talking about? Wh—"

"There's a bomb in the building. I'll get Kyle and the girls. You get up to that microphone and tell these people to clear out. I don't care what you say, just get them out of here and as far away from the building as possible. I'll meet you outside."

Susan stared at her in alarm, but didn't hesitate.

"Go," she said. "Go." Then she turned and headed for the podium.

Eight-fifty-five a.m.

Five precious minutes. It might be impossible to clear these people out that quickly, but Tara's only priority right now was Kelly and Kimberly.

She glanced around until she saw a sign pointing to the men's room. It was located to the right side of the lobby, down a narrow hallway.

Tara pushed past an elderly couple, telling them to leave the building, *now,* then moved into the hallway beyond an emergency exit and on toward the restroom.

She was only steps away from it when someone grabbed her from behind and stuck a gun barrel to her head, abruptly pulling her to the side.

"Well now, cutie-pie, nice to see you made it to the party. Me and you got some unfinished business to attend to."

Carl Maddox wrapped his arm around Tara's waist and dragged her toward the emergency exit.

WHEN THE SECURITY MAN first saw Matt, his eyes went wide and he started fumbling for his sidearm.

Fortunately, Abernathy had given Matt his bureau credentials and Matt already had them out as he approached, quickly explaining who he was and what was going on.

The security man looked wary, as if trying to decide whether to believe the story or arrest him, and Matt had no idea which way he'd go.

"Do you want the lives of hundreds of people on your conscience?" Matt asked. "You can either be a hero or a scapegoat. It's up to you."

The security man thought about this, then said, "What do you want me to do?"

"Your radios aren't working," Matt told him. "I need you to round up your men and get those people out of the building ASAP. It's about to blow."

Without any further prompting, the security man headed toward the lobby. Matt was about to follow when he heard a door at the side of the building crash open and Tara stepped onto the sidewalk.

What the heck?

What was she doing?

He was about to call out to her when he saw Carl Maddox move in behind her, pressing a gun to her back.

Matt felt his heart go into his throat.

He didn't have a weapon, and if he tried to stop them, Tara might be hurt. First, he needed to find some cover. A simple turn of the head and Maddox would see him.

Quickly moving to the back of the security man's car, he hunkered down and watched as Carl nudged Tara into the street, motioning for her to cross it.

There was a multistory parking lot on the other side, and Matt immediately knew where they were headed.

He was taking her to Zane.

CARL PUSHED TARA INTO the elevator and pressed the button for the top floor, closing them inside.

"This is your lucky day, cupcake. Everything's in place and ready to go. And you get a front row seat to the fireworks."

Tara's chest was pounding, but it was rage that consumed her. All she could think about was Kelly and Kimberly. "You twisted—"

"Now, now, is that any way to talk to the future father of your children?"

"Future dead man," Tara said as the elevator kicked into gear. "The very near future."

"Oooh, I like it when you talk like that. You're getting me all hot and bothered." He reached over and hit the emergency button, bringing the car to a halt. "Maybe we should forget the fireworks and start making some of our own."

"Dream on, creep."

Carl chuckled. "You're acting like you have a choice in the matter." He pressed the gun to her head. "But my little friend here says you don't. And he's all too happy to introduce you to his big brother." His eyes went cold. "Get down on your knees."

Tara refused to budge. He'd have to kill her to get what he wanted.

"Down on your knees, you little—"

Tara spit in his face, then brought one of those knees up fast and hard into his groin. He huffed out a breath, his face churning in pain as he blindly struck out at her, knocking her against the wall.

But Tara whirled and swung, hitting him with all of her strength, then dove for the control panel and pulled on the emergency button.

As the elevator lurched into motion, Carl swore and twisted around, grabbing her by the neck. He slammed her against the wall again, and suddenly the world turned sideways.

Carl put a hand on her shoulder and shoved her to her knees, his back to the elevator doors.

His eyes red with fury, he brought the gun up. "Forget the fireworks, baby. You just signed your death certificate."

But before he could pull the trigger, the elevator bell *dinged,* and the doors slid open to reveal Matt standing behind them.

Matt struck without hesitation, two rapid blows to Carl's head and kidneys and the creep crumpled to the floor, out cold.

As Matt retrieved Carl's gun, Tara let out a long, relieved breath before falling into his arms. "Oh, thank God, thank God."

"Abernathy must be here by now," Matt said. "Take the stairs and tell him where I am. I have to stop Zane before he has a chance to punch that detonator."

MATT DIDN'T HAVE TIME to deal with Carl, so he simply pressed the elevator button and let the doors close him inside and take him down to the first floor.

By the time the idiot woke up, he'd be surrounded by federal agents.

Holding the gun at his side, Matt moved to the scarred glass doors separating the elevator from the parking lot. He was on the top floor, and outside was an open-air view of the blacktop jammed up with cars.

It took him only a moment to find the one he was looking for: a shiny black Humvee, parked hastily toward the Performing Arts Center.

He couldn't be sure, of course, but his gut told him he had the right car. He had parked next to it in The Brotherhood's compound.

Slipping out the doors, he moved into a crouch behind a nearby sedan, shifting his gaze to a digital clock on the side of an adjacent building.

Eight-fifty-nine a.m.

If Zane stuck to his plan, he'd be pressing that detonator in exactly one minute, and Matt didn't have a second to waste.

Staying low, he darted across the lot and took cover behind another sedan. The Hummer was only a few yards away from him now, and he could see the driver's window from here.

Zane was behind the wheel, his concentration centered on the Performing Arts Center building, a small black box in his left hand. The detonator was radio controlled, which meant that Zane would have to cancel the cell phone jammer before he used it. Matt had a feeling that switch had already been flipped.

It's now or never, he thought.

Bringing Carl's gun up, he got to his feet and moved as quickly and as silently as possible, making a straight line for Zane.

But just as he reached the car's window, a shotgun ratcheted behind him and a familiar voice said, "You can stop right there, Mr. FBI."

Matt froze in place.

"Drop the weapon," Imogene said, her voice shaky.

Matt did as told, then slowly raised his hands as Zane gave him a once-over.

"Glad you could join us, soldier. I was just telling Mother what a shame it was we wouldn't get to see your face when the building blows. So having you here means a lot to me."

"It don't mean a darn thing to me," Imogene said.

"Just trigger that contraption already, so I can waste this piece of government garbage."

Matt felt a chill go down his spine. He couldn't believe he'd let this old lunatic dupe him. And a jumpy one at that. He could tell by the quaver in her voice that she'd fire that scattergun at the slightest provocation.

He glanced again at the clock on the adjoining building.

Nine a.m.

Zane smiled at him now, his thumb moving toward the detonator's trigger. "By the time they dig all the bodies out of the rubble," he said, "The Brotherhood will have a brand-new home in a brand-new state, and Whitestone won't quite know what hit it." He paused. "Like I always say, 'We hold the power.'"

Matt was no longer listening to him. His gaze was burning Zane's hand and he knew that if he didn't think of something fast, it would be over. Zane would win.

Tara was down there somewhere, trying to flag Abernathy, rushing frantically back to the building to save her sister and brother-in-law and those two little girls who meant so much to her. And he knew that he had failed her. That in the one crucial, final moment, the moment that meant everything, he had failed to fulfill his promise to her.

All he could see was her face. Bruised but beautiful. The face of an angel.

His angel.

And as Zane's thumb descended toward the button, Matt did the only thing he could think of.

He moved.

A single step sideways.

And just as he'd hoped—just as he'd prayed for—the sudden motion rattled Imogene and she reacted, letting loose both barrels of the shotgun.

By the time she fired, however, Matt had ducked well out of the way, and the charge rocketed forward, hitting Zane in the neck and chest, blowing a hole clean through him.

He was dead before Imogene even realized what she'd done, and Matt knocked the shotgun out of her hands as he lunged for the detonator, fearing it might tumble to the ground and accidentally trigger.

He caught it with the tips at his outstretched fingers, just in time to see Imogene's ravaged, grief-stricken eyes and hear her high, shrill wail.

TARA HAD BEEN TOO BUSY trying to help evacuate the building to pay any attention to the time.

She had no idea where Susan was, or Kyle and the twins, but when the last man, woman and child were safely outside and racing across the street, she saw the clock on the side of the building.

Nine-oh-three a.m.

It was past the deadline, yet the arts center was still in one piece.

Had Matt succeeded? Had he managed to stop Zane?

Tara got her answer when she glanced toward the top level of the parking lot and saw him standing at the cement barrier, waving at her, grinning from ear to ear, a small black box in his hand.

She'd never been so happy to see someone in her entire life. A grateful smile on her face, she returned Matt's wave, thinking how much she loved him.

Suddenly unable to control herself, her knees went weak and she stumbled to the sidewalk, an overwhelming feeling of joy rushing through her, tears filling her eyes.

As she sank to the curb, she buried her head in her hands, letting the tears flow and all the pain and worry of the past few hours drain from her body.

A small voice said, "Aunt Tara? Are you okay?"

She looked up to see Kelly and Kimberly standing in front of her now, Susan behind them with her hands on their small shoulders.

And with one last glance at Matt, Tara opened her arms wide and wrapped them in a loving embrace.

Chapter Twenty-Three

It took several days to round up Zane's soldiers.

When the feds raided his compound, they found that it had been completely destroyed by explosives, leaving behind little more than piles of rubble.

But somewhere in that rubble, a computer hard drive was found that contained a database of the names of every member of The Brotherhood.

Imogene Zane and Carl Maddox were taken into custody at the crime scene. Rusty Zane and several of his compatriots were found in New Mexico, trying to sneak across the border. And when the arts center building had been swept by the bomb squad, they discovered that over a dozen different stress points had been booby trapped with high explosives, just waiting for detonation.

Tara and Matt became media darlings, news stations around the world calling them heroes. Movie deals were rumored, a reality show was proposed, and

Tara was even offered an on-camera job with one of the major networks.

But she declined them all. And so did Matt. All they wanted from this was time alone.

Time together.

WHEN THEY HAD THAT time, however, when the dust had settled and all the cameras were gone, as much as she tried not to, Tara couldn't help but wonder if their relationship was a mistake. There was no question in her mind that Matt was her soul mate, but he was still a cop, and she knew what kind of life that would be.

But then he surprised her.

Late one night, after they had made love, as they lay in the darkness of her bedroom, Matt absently ran a finger over the spot where her bruise had been.

And he said, "I'll give it up, you know."

She wasn't quite sure what he meant, and her confusion must have shown on her face.

"The job," he said. "If it means losing you, I'll give it up. I can go back to practicing law."

"You'd do that?"

"In a heartbeat."

Tara could feel her own heart swell. That Matt was willing to give up everything he'd worked for to be with her was more than she could ever ask.

"I don't ever want you to feel neglected," he said. "I don't ever want you to be alone. Our kids, either."

Kids, Tara thought.

She liked the sound of that.

Cousins to Kelly and Kimberly.

She put her arms around him and Matt kissed her. "But there's something I think you need to see," he said. "It'll help you finally put the past to rest."

Tara was surprised. And curious. "What?"

Matt pulled away from her and flicked on a lamp, then rose from the bed and moved across the room to a backpack he'd left in a chair. He dug around inside, then took out a small, battered notebook.

"Your cop friend gave this to me today. Lila Sinclair. She didn't think you'd want to talk to her, so she asked me to pass it along. Said she's been wanting to give it to you ever since the funeral."

The mention of Lila brought Tara's guard up. Some habits were hard to shake. "I don't understand. What is it?"

"Your father's journal."

"His…what?"

"She said you'd be surprised to know that he'd been keeping one for years. She said the entries are sparse, but there's no mistaking that they came from his heart."

Tara didn't know what to do with this news. Keeping a journal seemed so out of character for her father that she had a hard time believing it was true.

But when Matt handed the notebook to her, she immediately recognized the handwriting. The neat, no-nonsense lines.

As she leafed through it, she couldn't quite believe what she was reading. He'd begun writing it shortly after the divorce. It was both a confession and, in a way, a love song—a love song to her and Susan— words of regret, of missed opportunities, that reached up and wrapped themselves around her.

Her father had loved them. Had cared about them.

Had hated himself for his failure to express it.

Had hoped that she and Susan would one day forgive him and take him back into their lives.

As Tara closed the notebook and set it aside, she began to cry, her own feelings of regret taking hold.

"I should have gone to him," she said softly. "I should have given him a second chance."

Matt sat next to her then, pulled her into his arms, and as she cried against his shoulder, she knew with sudden clarity that it didn't matter what Matt did for a living. It was ridiculous to judge a person based on that.

She would learn to live with it.

He was a good man and she could no more expect him to change than she could her father.

She didn't want him to.
She loved him.
Because he was, and always would be, her Henry.

* * * * *

Harlequin offers a romance for every mood!
See below for a sneak peek from
our suspense romance line
Silhouette® Romantic Suspense.
Introducing HER HERO IN HIDING by
New York Times *bestselling author Rachel Lee.*

Kay Young returned to woozy consciousness to find that she was lying on a soft sofa beneath a heap of quilts near a cheerfully burning fire. When she tried to move, however, everything hurt, and she groaned.

At once she heard a sound, then a stranger with a hard, harsh face was squatting beside her. "Shh," he said softly. "You're safe here. I promise."

"I have to go," she said weakly, struggling against pain. "He'll find me. He can't find me."

"Easy, lady," he said quietly. "You're hurt. No one's going to find you here."

"He will," she said desperately, terror clutching at her insides. "He always finds me!"

"Easy," he said again. "There's a blizzard outside. No one's getting here tonight, not even the doctor. I know, because I tried."

"Doctor? I don't need a doctor! I've got to get away."

"There's nowhere to go tonight," he said levelly.

"And if I thought you could stand, I'd take you to a window and show you."

But even as she tried once more to pull away the quilts, she remembered something else: this man had been gentle when he'd found her beside the road, even when she had kicked and clawed. He hadn't hurt her.

Terror receded just a bit. She looked at him and detected signs of true concern there.

The terror eased another notch and she let her head sag on the pillow. "He always finds me," she whispered.

"Not here. Not tonight. That much I can guarantee."

Will Kay's mysterious rescuer protect
her from her worst fears?
Find out in
HER HERO IN HIDING
by New York Times *bestselling author*
Rachel Lee
Available June 2010
Only from Silhouette® Romantic Suspense

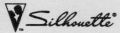

ROMANTIC
SUSPENSE

Sparked by Danger, Fueled by Passion.

NEW YORK TIMES AND *USA TODAY*
BESTSELLING AUTHOR

RACHEL LEE

BRINGS YOU AN ALL-NEW
CONARD COUNTY: THE NEXT GENERATION SAGA!

After finding the injured Kay Young on a deserted country
road Clint Ardmore learns that she is not only being hunted
by a serial killer, but is also three months pregnant.
He is determined to protect them—even if it means
forgoing the solitude that he has come to appreciate.
But will Clint grow fond of having an attractive woman
occupy his otherwise empty ranch?

Find out in

Her Hero in Hiding

Available June 2010 wherever books are sold.

Visit Silhouette Books at www.eHarlequin.com

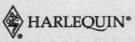

The Best Man in Texas
TANYA MICHAELS

Brooke Nichols—soon to be Brooke Baker—
hates surprises. Growing up in an unstable
environment, she's happy to be putting down
roots with her safe, steady fiancé. Then she meets
his best friend, Jake McBride, a firefighter and
former soldier who's raw, unpredictable and
passionate. With his spontaneous streak and
dangerous career, Jake is everything Brooke is
trying to avoid…so why is it so hard to resist him?

**Available June
wherever books are sold.**

"LOVE, HOME & HAPPINESS"

HARLEQUIN® *Blaze*™

is proud to present

New York Times bestselling author

Vicki Lewis Thompson

with a brand-new trilogy,
SONS OF CHANCE
where three sexy brothers
meet three irresistible women.

Look for the first book
WANTED!

*Available beginning in June 2010
wherever books are sold.*

---

red-hot reads

www.eHarlequin.com

HB79548

HARLEQUIN® *Romance.*

GIRLS' *Weekend in* **VEGAS**

Four friends, four dream weddings!

On a girly weekend in Las Vegas, best friends Alex, Molly, Serena and Jayne are supposed to just have fun and forget men, but they end up meeting their perfect matches! Will the love they find in Vegas stay in Vegas?

Find out in this sassy, fun and wildly romantic miniseries all about love and friendship!

Saving Cinderella! by MYRNA MACKENZIE
Available June

Vegas Pregnancy Surprise by SHIRLEY JUMP
Available July

Inconveniently Wed! by JACKIE BRAUN
Available August

Wedding Date with the Best Man
by MELISSA MCCLONE
Available September

www.eHarlequin.com

HR17663

LARGER-PRINT BOOKS!

GET 2 FREE LARGER-PRINT NOVELS

PLUS 2 FREE GIFTS!

HARLEQUIN®
INTRIGUE®

Breathtaking Romantic Suspense

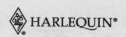
HARLEQUIN®

Showcase

Reader favorites from the most talented voices in romance

Save $1.00 on the purchase of 1 or more Harlequin® Showcase books.

On sale May 11, 2010

SAVE $1.00 on the purchase of 1 or more Harlequin® Showcase books.

Coupon expires Oct 31, 2010. Redeemable at participating retail outlets.
Limit one coupon per purchase. Valid in the U.S.A. and Canada only.

52609015

5 65373 00076 2   (8100)0 11651

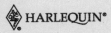
HARLEQUIN®

INTRIGUE

COMING NEXT MONTH

Available June 8, 2010

HICNMBPA0510